THE PRODUCT
OF MARCH

THE PRODUCT OF MARCH

DEVIANT BOOKS

NEW YORK

The Product of March Copyright © 2023 by Deviant Books.
All rights reserved.
Printed in the United States of America.
For information: contact@deviantpublishing.com

Editing by Alex Foster
Designed by Coverkitchen
ISBN: 9781733893312

*To the lovers, for giving me
the courage of my convictions.*

Preface

At some point in adolescence, the word *special* becomes a pejorative. At eleven years old, crying into my mother's arms, her profession of my uniqueness only made me feel worse. The pain of the constant estrangement I felt from my peers would not make sense for many years to come.

"What's wrong with me?" I cried in her arms, recalling how my teacher had made fun of me that day for being averse to the competitive nature of tug-o-war.

"Nothing's wrong with you, sweetie. Do you really want to be like everyone else? That's no fun."

I nodded silently, though being like everyone else meant I didn't have to be the laughing stock of the entire class.

Three years later, I was sitting at a library table in Union Vale Middle School with three classmates who I considered close friends. As I made my way to our lunch table, I saw one of them quickly pull a scrap of paper off the table and shove it into her pocket. I did not say anything, and neither did anyone else, but I could tell by their behavior that whatever was on that note most certainly had my name on it. They probably hoped I didn't notice. The fleeting image ingrained itself into my mind and consumed my thoughts for the rest of the period.

When the bell rang, I waited at the table until everyone had left. I watched my friends walk out of the library, and when I saw a flash of bright green fingernails deposit the note in the trash, I dug through the contents of the bin until my hand closed around the sweat-stained piece of paper. To my surprise, there were only three words on it: He is gay.

I understood what the note said, yet I could not comprehend if they meant it as a good or bad thing.

March

Nine years later, I was a business student at Boston College, where I quickly discovered I hated numbers. I switched my major to political science and marketing, then again to philosophy and communication and once more to international studies and psychoanalytic studies.

Due to the unconventional academic and extracurricular path I'd taken, more people knew about me than just my professors. I had worked my way through practically the whole college, and academics in every discipline seemed to know who I was. Late one evening, as I was walking home, the dean of students stopped me.

"Landon. You are the epitome of how a Jesuit education can change a life," he said.

"Oh." I shifted my books in my arms. "Thank you."

"You should speak to the office of first-year experience. They've built a freshman retreat and you are exactly what we have been looking for."

Eager for a sense of belonging, that's what I did. Sally and Brian at the office of first-year experience helped me craft a personal narrative for the retreat called 48 Hours. I practiced my speech with them for weeks before the first presentation in early September, reminding me how raw and honest my message was. We discussed how I had turned towards a combination of drugs, alcohol and the ROTC program when I felt utterly alone; how my parents' divorce drove me towards a robotic way of behaving, how I was plucked off Instagram and became a male model, then what happened when asteroid-sized obstacles started falling around me, trapping me in a burning circle of doom.

All of this made for an impactful story—so much so that it was regarded as the most receptive speech in the program's history. The addictions that made the story so compelling were normally not discussed at a Catholic school. Sally and Brian and I had made history, and we were proud of that.

The next year, while I was studying abroad in London, I had a Skype interview to become an orientation leader at Boston College. I had no summer prospects at the time but I was a planner; I planned everything. *Foresight is the key to a strong future. A strong future is the key to happiness.* The interviewing team was comprised of people I considered close friends and mentors, including Sally and Brian. I was excited to speak to them and confident that I could impress them. I was logistically stellar when it came to interviewing. Junior year was a pivotal time for securing internships, and I knew all the tips and tricks, including looking at the glowing green dot in the center of my MacBook. This way my future employers would feel as though I was looking at them instead of my own reflection.

"Hi Landon! Let's jump right into it," Sally said when the call started. The group wasted no time with their questions.

I nailed the first dozen questions, explaining the way to handle adversity with incoming freshmen, when to tackle an interpersonal problem myself and when to get an adult involved, and so forth. Then Sally asked, "What do you see as your greatest strength?" I glanced at the clock, away from the penetrating green dot, thinking it was too late in the interview for such a simple question.

It's been 38 minutes and 14 seconds. Colman and I have to catch a flight to Iceland at 20:34 at London Heathrow. The traffic is going to be extremely problematic.

My greatest strength was my ability to categorize and organize a given group of factors into a single cohesive unit to produce something that was extraordinarily detail-oriented and effective. I could synthesize and compile information like a professional. But for some reason, that's not what I said this time. Suddenly I could not find the green dot.

In all other interviews, I would proceed with my spiel with examples of when and how I demonstrated this ability, then wait for the smile or raised eyebrows indicating that my answer was impressive. I would chuckle and continue pulling from the bank of socially-accepted answers until the interview ended.

"Hello?" They repeated.

What do they mean 'Hello?' I just answered the question. Did we disconnect?

Bryan finally grabbed the camera and shook it, which pulled me out of a hypnotic state. I had not answered the question yet.

"Landon?"

"Yes, wow, I am so sorry about that. I lost connection there for a second. You'll have to excuse me; the Wi-Fi is shaky here."

"No worries. We're glad it is working properly now. I don't know if you heard us but we asked what you thought your greatest—"

"I love a lot of different types of people," I blurted out.

What did I just say?

"Can you repeat that?" Sally said, visibly trying to refrain from laughing after a moment of shock.

This time I did not hesitate. I repeated the same thing I had said before. It was like my mouth was fighting with my brain. I knew what I was trying to say but something opposite was happening. *Do I love a lot of different types of people?*

"And that's a strength?" she said as she pulled her paper and pen closer to her.

"That's correct. I would be a good candidate for this position because I love a lot of different type of people. That's what you need to be an Orientation Leader, isn't it?" I said, confused by my own answer. I had no idea why I was blushing.

"Do you have another strength that you would be willing to share with us?" Brian said.

"Not that I can think of," I responded quickly. *I am so going to be so screwed with this traffic.*

"Then..." Sally looked at Brian for some type of confirmation.

"That about wraps it up," Brian said.

"Oh, really? There's nothing else—"

"Nope, that is it. We will get back to you in about two weeks. This year is highly competitive but we think you would be a great fit for the program. We already know your story, after all," Brian said.

"Thank you—" I started, but Skype went dark.

Five days later, I received an email confirming that the office of first-year experience truly valued my time and my story, but were unable to offer me a spot as an orientation leader for the 2018 cohort. They knew my story; the gut-wrenching story that they asked me to craft and practice over and over with them just a semester earlier. They said it made a huge impact on the freshmen and gave them genuine hope that, regardless of the obstacles or family troubles they will face during their time at Boston College, there will always be someone who will want to help. They milked my story and used it in their program even after I left. I guess they didn't need me to deliver it anymore; I'd fulfilled my use.

My mom always said not to change who I am, but if I didn't, I was cast aside.

On March ninth, two days after the interview and almost

missing the flight to Iceland, I found myself riding shotgun in a Toyota Yaris as my brother drove into the Icelandic wilderness at 21:00 hours. We had come from our hotel, which was literally in the middle of nowhere, surrounded by piles of snow and large ice blocks. The hotel was immaculate, but the wind had nothing to break it and rushed against our sliding doors with such intensity that I thought the glass was going to break.

Twenty minutes earlier, I had a glass of whiskey with dinner. My brother insisted that a single drink could impair my ability to drive and he would not be able to trust me, especially after all the driving I'd done earlier that day. Colman will always be the responsible older brother…even though he was younger. As we drove past the barren plains and impeding mountains that absorbed the darkness, I relived the same experience with him as I had with Sally and Brian – my mouth kept moving, contrary to my brain.

"You know what I really want for my birthday?" I said out of nowhere, rushing towards Diamond Beach to see the Aurora Borealis.

"Oh god, I can only imagine," he laughed.

"I want a threesome."

"There it is! The true Landon North." He moaned, though audibly amused.

"I think that would be a great gift from the universe, don't you? It is my twenty-first birthday after all, so I think there should be some universal mandate that makes something extra special happen. It's only right."

"I can think of a few other gifts I would prefer, but if you really want to enlighten me, the floor is all yours."

"You know what else… it doesn't even have to be with two girls." I felt my shoulders tense and draw closer to my ears. Blood filled my face, and I was glad it was already so dark outside.

He paused. Colman had always been more careful with his

words than me, and I was accustomed to these types of silences.

"How would it be a threesome if you didn't have two girls?"

"Well, I don't know. I was thinking, like, there are all these theories and, you know, like, how can someone say they're straight when they haven't tried anything else? Historically speaking there were so many cultures that had like huge orgies and all that," I mumbled.

"You don't want a threesome then? You want an orgy?"

"No, I don't know, maybe, eventually, possibly, but not right now. I have like four things left on my bucket list…"

"Your sexual bucket list?"

"Yes."

"I'm surprised you haven't had a threesome," he said after another brief silence.

"Me too. But what I'm saying is that it might be good for me, or like, everyone, to try something new. Like roommates can have a threesome together, right? I think that would be the epitome of friendship, you know what I am saying?"

"I don't, actually. But if you want to explain, I can't possibly go anywhere so I am stuck with you." He turned down the radio volume as we hurtled towards Skaftafell National Park.

"I don't know. Maybe it's not a good idea."

"I think you should do what you want to do," he said plainly.

This time I paused.

"I was in a psychoanalytic class this year and we studied Freud. Freud actually believed that the human species is, by default, bisexual and that it's the rigid social construct that restricts most sexual experimentation."

"Why did he say that?" Colman said.

"I think it's because each gender offers something inherently unique to society. I'm not arguing that women have a place in society that men can't have or vice versa, but I would argue that women are naturally more caring and emotional.

Everyone needs this in their life to prevent what Freud called an ego split. He also said that men share some innate bond that cannot be replicated by women and sexually engaging with that bond only heightens and solidifies that which we spend our whole lives trying to find. It really is only society that tells people to be straight. Freud theorized that this straightness is needed to maintain the longevity of the human race. That's not to say that everyone would go gay, of course not—all I am saying is that it's an interesting concept, you know... to maybe think about."

Colman paused for longer this time. He was thinking of something inherently relevant to say.

"There are a lot of celebrities that experiment with that kind of stuff, I guess."

"Exactly!" I yelled. "All I am saying is that how can I say I'm straight if I've never even had the other option before? Like, during post games at BC, I just sit around and listen to the drunk talk that happens between my roommates. The topics of sex and sexuality always come up and I never say anything but I feel like I can't be the only one who thinks about this, right? All these guys talk about how much pussy they want to get the next night or what happened to their dicks earlier that evening. I just don't think that makes a lot of sense, like, they are talking about their own penises with their friends and yet if that were to go beyond 'just talking', that is gay. Yet the whole thing is homoerotic," I spat out.

"You've thought about this a lot?"

"Well, no. I mean, sure. Well...I think about a lot of things, this is just one of them. I don't even know why it came up. Never mind, let's just forget about it," I said, bringing my face back towards the passenger window.

"I totally agree with you though."

"You do?"

"Yes, I do. You know I would tell you if I thought you were

wrong, but I don't think so in this case. I think you're thinking in a rational and logical manner, and if that's something you want to experiment with, I support you 100%."

"You do?" I repeated.

"You act as if you don't believe me."

"You support what I just said?" I restated, unable to believe my own liberal stance on sexual orientation. *Growing up in a family of conservatives made it difficult to even think about these things.*

"I wouldn't want to do that myself, but we're two completely different people. You can ask me the same thing however many times you want but my answer is not going to change. If it's something you want to do then do it. I told you I didn't support your decision to do all those drugs during sophomore year, didn't I?"

"Yes."

"Sexual experimentation is much better than experimenting with drugs, as long as you use protection." Then he reached for the volume knob, turning Runaway by Kanye West back up.

After another ten minutes we arrived at Glacier Lagoon. There were eight cars in the parking lot adjacent from the lagoon. As soon as we arrived, Colman went to work downloading an app that allowed him to photograph the Aurora Borealis. We could see them in the distance but he said we wouldn't be able to really see them until around 2200 hours.

We snacked on a tube of Digestives we had brought from London and waited. Colman dozed off, and I played Odesza's *A Moment Apart* album on low. I felt like I was back on ecstasy in sophomore year. I was sitting in a car in Iceland with my brother, who just said he would support my outlandish idea, about to witness the Northern Lights. Eerily, at 2200 exactly, a ripple of green appeared in the eastern sky and my pseudo-ecstasy reached its climax. My brother and I stepped out to watch more bands of light join in. I couldn't stop smiling.

One week after Iceland, I was sitting in my exceedingly-small Queen Mary University dorm room alone, again, with the window open. The breeze was getting warmer but the London air was still damp and bone-soaking. I had just finished a dissertation on pragmatics and its relation to the establishment of power hierarchies in dialogue, as well as an essay for my Popular Theater and Performance class. Neither essay was due until April, but I had planned ahead, knowing I wouldn't have the motivation to finish the essays on the various trips I also had planned. There was a teacher's strike since the second week of classes and while every other student was basking in their freedom, I had come there to study. To learn. To better myself. To plan. To create a future. To succeed. *People would see I was a success.*

I was going to send the linguistics dissertation to the White House as my writing sample. I had coveted the idea of The White House Internship since I was six years old and my application would finally be strong enough, as long as my grades – even with striking teachers – held to their usual standard. I wanted to prove to the office of speechwriting that I could research and compile an entire project in less than a week. At 19:14 hours, after nine hours of writing, a five-mile run that morning, and a mid-day lift, I finally granted myself the ability to relax.

I opened my laptop to reward myself with a movie, queued up iTunes to see what movies were available to rent, and as the VPN booted up, I made myself my first drink.

I had taken a bartending class in Boston the previous summer and had become fascinated with mixology. I had also discovered around that same time what would become my favorite drink—an Italian Daiquiri—which I had found at a restaurant called Copa in Boston. The recipe is two-parts Clement Creole Shrub Rum, one-part St. George's Spiced Pear liquor, two dashes of Angostura bitters, half an ounce of freshly squeezed lime juice, and half an ounce of Foro Amoro. It's an aperitif, which is supposed to be drank after dinner, but screw it. I watched hungrily as the swirling oranges and reds poured out of the shaker.

I cleaned my small desk, as a good bartender does, so the drops of alcohol wouldn't stain the wood. The VPN had connected successfully and American iTunes movies displayed themselves proudly on the LED screen. My search would have to be limited to a rental because my father had just called me out for the outrageous charges on his credit cards for movies I'd bought. I scrolled through the popular movie category, but because most of the new movies had just been released, they were all $14.99 with no option to rent. Maybe I could buy just one more and he wouldn't notice. I kept scrolling until I saw a film to rent: Call Me By Your Name.

I have heard that title somewhere before...

It was on a date in Copenhagen four weeks prior. One of my best friends, Francine, was studying in Copenhagen but she had to work during one of the evenings I was visiting. She decided to set me up with one of her friends so I wouldn't have to wander around the city by myself. Francine reserved us a table at a famous ramen restaurant, where she had been waitressing to put her through the semester, then Frankie and I left for the evening. Frankie was leaving for the Arctic Circle the next morning and told me that it wouldn't be a late night for her. We had no idea what to do in the cold, so as we were passing by a theater, I suggested we see a movie. The Disaster Artist was playing and neither of us had seen it. We talked cinema while we waited in line for our tickets. I asked her what one of her favorite movies was. She paused and picked a Twix from the candy rack.

"Right now, it would have to be Call Me By Your Name."

"Cool, I have never heard about that one, what's that about?" I asked but never got an answer. We were immediately shuffled into the theater and Frankie got a free Twix. I would have never watched Call Me By Your Name had Frankie explained to me the premise.

Without looking at the plot summary on iTunes, I clicked rent. The movie was almost three gigabytes and with the slow and spotty wireless connection in my room, I knew it was going to take a while before I was able to watch it. I made myself another drink. This time, I went straight for whiskey. My two bottles of Knob Creek Rye were sitting right behind the other alcohols in my collection, and a bottle of sweet vermouth was resting next to the twins. I pulled another martini glass from the shelf, dropped in two cherries, added one-part sweet vermouth, two shakes of bitters and two-parts whiskey. I stirred it and had myself a stellar Manhattan.

I checked the time remaining for the movie download. Twenty minutes lent me an ample drinking interval. With the amount of work I had completed that day, my first Manhattan was savored but empty in a matter of five minutes. With fifteen left to load, I switched to an Old Fashioned. I got the sugar cube, soaked it in bitters, ground it up with the muddler, added a teaspoon of cherry juice, cut one slice of an orange and muddled that concoction together. I then got the jigger, filled it up twice with GlenDronach 12-Year-Old Original and sat for the remaining ten minutes watching the circle go around and around in the top right corner of iTunes, already hammered but enjoying myself nonetheless.

I premade a second Old Fashioned and did not care that I was already seven shots of liquor into my evening. The time was 21:41 and I wobbled as I carried my computer to my bed. I pressed the play button and knew, in those first five minutes, that Call Me By Your Name would rank amongst the most beautiful movies of the year. By the end of the two hours, nine shots deep, I cried with Elio as he sat by the fireplace in his home. He was me and I was him because we were thoroughly alone in the end.

That March was life changing. It presented me with a sequence of events that not only changed how I looked at the world but also how I positioned myself in it. I spent many days and nights in my Queen Mary dorm room wondering where I was going to end up, what I was going to do, and who I was going to end up with. My mother's words, *Do you really want to be like everyone else*, appeared in my head so often that they became one of my closest friends, showing up to talk to me over and over again. I was special but I would just be better than everyone else, not different.

I was a student at Boston College to show the world I was smart.

I was a fashion model to show the world I was attractive.

I volunteered in hospitals and foster homes to show the world I was kind.

I interned in the United States Senate to show the world I was ambitious.

I traveled to show the world I was cultured.

I was social to show the world I was loved by others.

I would succeed. Success was paramount.

Until that March, I had shown the world so many things but not once shown anything real. I was taught to simply adapt to the environment, rather than try to change it. To this day, I don't know which event started the multiplication to come, or if it was the totality of the sequence which changed me, but I began to see how special I truly was. *I would succeed. Success was paramount.* I wanted to be a success in the eyes of those around me but I secretly romanticized about how one day I might be able to feel special, internally. Even better, in the one-in-a-million chance I was lucky enough, I would meet someone who would accept me as me and maybe *just maybe* they would feel I was special too.

By the end of that March in London, that one person was two.

March -
Saint Patrick's Day

"Landon," Jake said through the phone.

"That is my name," I responded lightheartedly.

"We are going out tonight. I know you just left but I changed my mind. It's Saint Patrick's Day and we should have gotten drunk today instead of strolling through Covenant Garden."

"Or, and listen to this because this is another always another option—" I began.

"The answer is no. Whatever excuse you have prepared to stay in your room, the answer is no. I already told Abby and Steven we would go out with them and if we order donuts one more time this week, I will have spent over a hundred dollars on them in the last month alone. I will not subject myself to that."

"Dude, come on, can't we just make some whiskey sours in one of our rooms? You can come here or I'll bring a bottle back to LSE."

I'd had a photoshoot the day before which lasted fourteen hours, and I was still recovering. I was willing to do anything except be social and drink.

"Nope, sorry. Abby said a lot of people are going out tonight and I told them we would join. I'll meet you outside LSE in 40 minutes. Our call time is nine so we can get some low-key drinks before if you want. There's a bar I've wanted to try."

"Ugh!" I groaned knowing I would not win. "What should I wear?"

"They said this place is kind of like a dive bar so use your discretion. I'm going to dress up but only because I want to. And before you say anything, I already know I'm going to end up regretting getting fancy but I do not care. You don't have to tell me."

"Fine," I huffed.

"39 minutes remaining. Better get your ass over here," he laughed, ending the call.

I stared at my closet hoping some sort of fashion inspiration would come to me. I could dress up, but I didn't want to copy Jake. Plus, he was right, he would end up regretting his choice when he was drunk and his collar was too tight.

I looked longingly between my rack of long-sleeved shirts and piles of t-shirts. *Come on, just pick something.* At the bottom of the t-shirts was a bright yellow one I brought to England for this very occasion. I held it up in front of myself in the waist-high mirror. The Budweiser logo was right where a front pocket would be. On the back, the vintage Eagle unfurled its wings across the width of my shoulders as its talons gripped a beer tower. The image was the antithesis of who I was – it was perfect.

I smiled at my reflection. *Thank you, baby Jesus.* This is exactly what I needed. I may look like a walking advertisement for American consumerism, but the moment everyone gets drunk and the bar gets crowded, I'd make my famous Irish-exit and be back in my room before I knew it.

I ran to the Mile End Tube station and was at London School of Economics in twenty minutes flat. It was still cold out, but a few drinks would fix that. We would have plenty of time to get drunk before I'd have to interact with people.

"What's up?" Jake asked as he emerged from his dorm. "Nice shirt."

"Thanks," I said as we started toward Chinatown. "Dude, I cannot believe we are almost done with this semester. We're going to be seniors next year."

"Next year is going to be so fun. Let's make a promise right now that we'll throw a shit-ton of parties in our Mod."

"Absolutely," I laughed, trying not to think about the reality of how busy work and school would keep me. "It's going to be so easy to pull all those freshman and sophomore girls."

"I don't think we even know the half of it. So where do you want to go first? We still have a while before we have to meet Abby, so I was thinking maybe a little upscale to start the night and then we slowly descend into the shadows."

"So that is why you got dressed up! You think I'll be able to get into somewhere nice with what I'm wearing though?"

"Not if you were a regular human being, but we all know you can charm your way into anything."

I smiled. Playing a part was my specialty. I skipped forward to a classy-looking sign a few meters ahead. At the door we were greeted not by a burly man in a trench coat or football jacket like American bouncers, but by a young man smaller than me, and definitely gay.

"IDs please." He smirked, eying me.

I looked away and was afraid Jake saw the interaction but he was too concerned with the cocktail dresses flouncing in and out of the door.

"We're sorry..." the bouncer started, focusing on the yellow t-shirt obscured beneath my jacket.

"We're only staying for a little bit, I know the shirt is a problem. We'll be out of here in twenty minutes," I smiled, gently placing my hand on his and looking directly into his eyes as he handed me back my ID, just long enough to send a message.

The corner of his mouth twitched, "Hmm you are looking

for a good night," and then watched me disappear into the darkness.

After we checked our coats, we descended to the lower bar and entered into a new world. The chandeliers were made of antlers, and sheep and cow skins were pinned on the walls and ceilings. The high-tops were old barrels and in every nook were massive tables placed for the random college reunion, bachelorette party or business deal. I was visibly out of place the minute I descended the steps—even the bartenders looked nicer than me. Everyone was insanely attractive. I should have listened to the bouncer.

"Dude, I made the wrong call," I said as I brought my hand up to adjust my hair.

"Believe me, you look fine," Jake said.

"Are you looking around us right now? You could pass for at least 25, but not me."

"They let you in, didn't they?"

We held our position at the shoulder-wide spot at the bar, among the flurry of upper-class studs and ladies around us, tipping the first drink down easily. After another whisky sour and espresso martini, I saw movement in one of the nooks currently occupied by a massive group of screaming women. It was too dark to see much, but they were without a doubt celebrating a bachelorette party. They were too drunk to be functioning, much less be in a place like this. I was about to make a joke when two women bolted from the table and raced towards us; thinking they were headed to the bar, I moved out of their way. Instead, they grabbed my biceps and pulled me close enough so that the bachelorette could plant the most slobbery kiss of my life onto my lips. They were gone before I could process what happened.

"I had a gut feeling that was going to happen," Jake smirked after glancing up from his phone. I looked back towards the table, where the women were now gesturing for me to join them.

"Go ahead. I know you want to!" Jake said. "I'm going to call Abby right now anyway because she's not getting my texts. I'll be right back down. Don't take anyone back to Queen Mary or I'm going to be stuck by myself for the rest of the night!"

"Just text me when you know where Abby is," I said as he disappeared.

I took a deep breath and settled into my rhythm. I could do this in my sleep.

"Hiya," I said as I reached the table.

"Do you want to take a seat or are you going to stand over us like some creep?" one of the women slurred.

"My friend and I were just about to leave to meet up with some friends at another bar but I wanted to come over and thank you for the kiss. It means a lot." I placed a hand over my heart.

My comment received a unanimous "Oooh" from the table.

"Was that your boyfriend?" The bride-to-be asked, standing to face me. The table giggled.

The mention of a boyfriend made my face immediately turn bright red. *Thank God it's so dark down here.*

"If I had a boyfriend, would that make me more or less interesting given that I'm standing here in front of you?" I sipped my drink, maintaining my gaze with the woman over the rim of my glass.

I received another round of "Oooh"s from the table. Now it was the woman's turn to blush. I didn't hesitate, leaning in and lifting her chin with my finger to kiss her. This time a round of excited squeals erupted from the table, followed by a series of yelps throughout the bar. I pulled back and looked at the face I just kissed to see her eyes were still closed.

"But like I said," I whispered, "My so-called boyfriend and I have to go meet some friends at another bar." Before she could respond, I turned to address the rest of the table. "You ladies have a good rest of your night." I smiled and turned for the door, my heart pounding.

Near the bottom of the stairs, Jake quickly gestured to me that it was time to go. I nodded from across the room, afraid he somehow knew about the woman's comment. It didn't mean anything—it wasn't my fault.

A round of applause cleared me a path to the stairs. I smiled, somewhat embarrassed but mostly pleased that my performance had the desired effect—the effect, of course, being the illusion of a masculine, heterosexual character. As I started up the stairs, I glanced down to see the woman raise a small glass in my direction.

"You are unbelievable. Did you invite her to meet us any-where?" Jake laughed.

"I just left it as is," I said nonchalantly.

"Come on. Let's grab our coats and go meet Steven; he says there's a wicked line forming."

It took another ten minutes to get to the designated bar, the line outside wrapped around the block. The three drinks were hitting me, and I felt the inevitable tingling around my eyes. The night was about to get a whole lot more fun. As Jake and I headed toward the back of the line, I made eye contact with perhaps the most beautiful woman I'd ever seen. The world stood still. I almost walked right into an oncoming car, when an arm pulls me back into the safety of the masses. Abby, Steven and the rest of the Boston College crew gathered at the back of the line.

"Trying to get killed?" Abby shouted over the buzz of the crowd.

"This line!" I groaned, happy to change the subject.

"We told you it would be packed!"

"I know, I know, Jake has been telling me to move my butt all night," I responded as I shook all the guys' hands.

"Well we're all here now, so get ready to have a fun night," Steven grinned.

"Amen," Jake and I said in unison. We looked at each other and burst out laughing. This was not the first time we'd finished each other's sentence, so to speak.

"And that's why you two are the best friends of Boston College," Dillon said.

In the bar, I immediately felt at home. This was the type of place we liked. It was too loud to hear your friends talk, too dark and flashy to know where you were in space and the floors were at a college-approved level of stickiness. I could already smell the sweat clinging to the bodies and heat radiating from behind the bar.

"Let's go down to the lower level!" Jake yelled to the group.

After we descended the first set of steps, something fell on my head. I swung my hands up instinctually and felt my fist meet flesh.

"You need to relax," came a woman's voice, tinged with a sweet accent—maybe French? My heart sank—did I just punch her? I imagined the phone call with my parents: *Dad, I got deported from London because I hit a girl in a club.*

I turned to see that it was the girl from the line, holding her shoulder and laughing. She was wearing a big St. Patrick's Day hat which was what had just fallen on me. Her eyes were emerald green and shining. The light was coming from within them, not being reflected back. Something was glowing in my peripherals, and when I find the strength to pull myself away from her eyes, the shining objects were her teeth. The moment lasted probably three seconds, but felt bigger than the rest of my life combined.

"Or how about I buy you a drink and then we can go from there?" I managed.

"How about you follow your friends and try to have a good night without this hat," she said, gently touching the tip of the drooping shamrock.

"My night might get worse if I can't buy a beautiful girl a

drink," I said, caught off guard by my own confidence.

"It might also get worse if I start screaming because you punched me." She smirked and then pulled her friend down the stairs and past the struggling hoard of Boston College students still attempting to make their way down.

"What was that about?" Jake yelled over the noise as I watched her weave her way through the crowd.

"I accidentally hit her."

"What?" he shouted, cupping his ear.

"I accidentally hit her... or something!" But he still couldn't hear me.

"She was cute, you should go for it."

"Believe me, she is not into it."

On the lower level we had some shots of Bushmills whisky with the rest of the group—it was Saint Patrick's Day, after all. The drinks came one after another, and the flow of people kept increasing. Three shots later, I noticed that the girl and her friend were engaged in a conversation with three noticeably older men. They had to be 35 and looked out of place in the crowd. I can tell by the women's body language that they are not engaged at all. Green-eyes kept checking her phone, which the three guys definitely did not notice, while her friend stifled a yawn.

Jake interrupted my drunk analysis and handed me another shot from over my shoulder. Green-eyes' friend turned in my direction, making direct eye contact with me. She smiled at me, like so many other people since I arrived, but nothing was like the smile from Green-eyes. This smile was platonic in the very definition of the word. It's a look you'd give someone passing them in the street. I smiled back, swallowing the shot, which only made me spill the alcohol on my shirt. I quickly attempted to play it off like nothing happened, but she was already laughing at me from across the packed dancefloor. I smiled and began to turn away when she slyly tipped her head in her friend's direction.

I had been in this situation too many times to misinterpret what she was trying to say. I nodded my head up and down like a broken bobblehead—*Yes, I am interested in Green-eyes.* She brought her hand to her mouth and feigned surprise, which made me laugh. I pointed at the men and raised my eyebrows, trying to indicate their role in all of this. The girl rolled her eyes and shrugged. After what seemed like an eternity, Green-eyes noticed her friend was no longer engaging in the conversation and followed her gaze back to me—standing creepily on the other side of the floor. She just smiled. I took that as my invitation to join the group, but as I walked over, the girls exchanged panicked looks. Green-eyes slapped her friend, who just kept laughing.

"Bonjour," I said directly to Green-eyes. It was a risk, but something told me she was French.

"Bro, you just interrupted the conversation. How about you get out," the beefy Brooklyn dude said.

This wasn't the first time I'd been in a situation like this, and I knew how to roll with the punches. I turned to the guy and put my hands out, palms up, like I didn't know what he meant.

"Excusez-moi? Parlez-vous Francais?" I said quizzically.

"Is this kid with you?" Brooklyn asked, tapping the other two guys for backup.

"Pardon?" I repeated.

I turned my back on the three guys and looked directly at the enchanting smile directed my way, daring her to make a definitive response.

"Yes, I am so sorry. My friend here must need something," she said. Now I knew I picked the right accent. Her voice flowed around her like a wisp of smoke.

"Tell us where you go tonight. Us New Yorkers know how to have a good time," Brooklyn said as he fist-bumped his friends. I smiled at them as they walk away.

"I came over as quick as I could," I said to the girls. "I

could see that I needed to save you from the conversation."

"We were actually talking about interesting things!" Green-eyes said.

"Like how much protein powder you can snort in one sitting?"

"How did you know?" She laughed again and this time the room really did spin. The noise was fluid and unbroken, all a single sound and pitch. It was so pure, my mind did not register when she stopped.

Her friend stood up. "I am going to get a—"

"No, you are not. This American punched me and almost took my hat earlier. Now you want to leave me with him? What kind of a friend are you?"

"The kind of friend that got him over here," she smiled.

"What makes you think I even wanted him over here?"

"Sidonie, don't be so—"

"Sidonie?" I interrupted. "A beautiful name for an even more beautiful girl."

"I am going to get a drink now," her friend said. Sidonie tried to grab her arm but she broke free and strutted towards the bar.

She sighed and faced me, giving in. "Parlez-vous Francais?"

"That was pretty much the only thing I remember from Cannes. I wish I could speak more. However, if it's any consolation, I can snort a lot of protein powder," I said.

"That was cute what you did. I should have said no and seen what they would have done to you instead."

"If you said no then you wouldn't be getting a free drink."

"What makes you think I want you to buy me a drink?"

"You told those guys yes, now I get to repay the favor."

The name Sidonie could not fit anyone more perfectly. Everything about her was star-like, from her gleaming eyes to her tinkling laugh. Her smile was the best part because it came from her eyes instead of her mouth.

"One drink," she said, looking over my shoulder for her friend, "Do you use that line on everyone, it is a overworked, no?"

"If it makes you feel better, I would be glad to buy your friend a drink as well. And no, I have only ever used that line once."

"That would make me feel better, but right now I can't find her. Uh, she just left me here with you!"

"The man who saved you from a boring conversation and now is going to get you free alcohol just for telling me your name, where you're from and what your favorite color is? You know... all the important stuff."

"Boy," she said bluntly. "The boy who just saved me."

"Is that an admission that I did actually save you?"

"One drink. Then I'll leave and you can buy someone else a drink. I know how this works." I could tell that she really did know how this works. But this was different—I really wanted to talk to her.

When I brought her a gin and tonic, she took one sip and then shoved the rest at me. "There, you've bought me a drink. Now I have to go."

"Wait," I begged, desperate now. If she walked away forever, I didn't know what I'd do. "Please stay."

With a heavy sigh, she sat back down. "Why?"

To my delight, the conversation was natural. We talked for five hours about school, life, work, travel and our hopes and dreams. Not once did she let me see who she really was as a person. She gave me just enough information so that I could pretend I understood her.

She was from Paris and was in London for spring break. When I asked her what she was studying or how old she was, she responded by asking me to guess. I guessed a million different things that morning, but each time she shrugged her shoulders and asked, "Why?" Not only had I never talked to a woman like this before, but I don't think I had ever met someone like her before. I was mesmerized.

"Hello, man," her friend said to me at 0500 hours.

"Are you referring to me?" I said.

"Yes, and I am here to tell you that Sidonie and I have to go home now. We both drank too much tonight."

"Not me. He only bought me one drink," she said, pouting.

"I would have bought you however many drinks you wanted if you asked."

"I'm only joking," she said before leaning in to kiss me warmly on the cheek. "Hannah's right, I must go now. I had a nice night and want to thank you again for not punching me a second time."

"You can repay me by giving me your number," I said quickly as she collected her things.

"Uh!" Hannah groaned. "Just give him your number and let's go. We have a taxi waiting."

"I'll give you my number if you give me something first," Sidonie whispered.

"What do you want to trade?"

"What do you think would be a fair trade?"

"How about my name?" I said.

"Your name?"

"You have not asked me for my name at all tonight. If I trade my name for your number, then you can call the cops if your shoulder starts hurting later. Or you can send your friends from New York after me."

Instead of saying anything else, she snatched my phone out of my hand and quickly typed in her number. "You may have to add +33 before the number if you don't have an international phone," she said, standing in front of me. I saved it quickly.

"Thank you," I said, leaning in to kiss her. She stopped me three inches away from her face and placed two fingers on my lips.

"And when I leave here and go tell the cops that I got punched tonight, what name should I tell them?"

"Landon," I whispered.

"I will make sure to repeat that nice and clearly for them. Goodnight, Landon," she said, draping her yellow jacket over her arm as she walked through the exit.

Jake found me ten minutes later and we left Waxy O'Connor's for the first and final time that semester. I wouldn't have wanted to go there again for a night of drinking with friends—the place was sacred now, reserved for Sidonie.

March 18ᵗʰ

I didn't want to make a drink for fear of obscuring my still pristine memory of her—the precise curl of her sweet French accent, the sheen of her dark hair on her shoulders in the dimly-lit bar. Instead I lay on my bed staring at the ceiling, holding her image in my mind.

My phone rang sharply, shattering the dreamy bubble I'd created.

"Hello?"

"What are you doing?" Jake said quickly. "I'm at the Saint Patrick's Day parade. Don't ask me why they have it the day after Saint Patrick's Day but it's really cool if you want to come out."

Not a chance. "I actually might see that girl from last night. She has flight back to Paris tonight and she invited me to Camden Market before she leaves. It was probably a drunk invite but I'm going to check anyway." I couldn't remember the last time I told Jake no.

"No worries dude, I just wanted to give you the option. When you get back from Camden let me know, and if we aren't tired then let's do something."

"You know I will." But I couldn't think that far ahead.

"Get this money, baby!" he shouted.

"Get this money, baby!" I repeated, laughing as he hung up the phone.

I regretted not drinking water between cocktails last night. The base of my skull was throbbing along with my heartbeat thanks to drunk Landon, who thinks he's a superhero. Not to mention Sidonie never responded to the text I sent late last night. Did adding the +33 screw it up? I sent the same message minus the country code, but the headache was so bad that I put my phone back on the dresser and closed my eyes.

I'd only been like this once before, obsessing over some girl's text message, and that was in high school. It was effortless being with Sidonie last night. She was the Athena of the bar. I felt small and unworthy in her presence. Every guy around me stared at her when she started laughing. Two or three groups even approached her while she was talking to me, asking if they could buy her a drink—exactly as I had done. It annoyed me, but at the same time, I felt reassured that I had made the right choice interrupting those Brooklyn guys.

I was about to give in to my despair and take a nap when my phone started ringing. Adrenaline surged into every nerve in my body. I leapt out of bed and answered the call without even looking at the ID.

"This is Landon," I panted.

"Yes, I know who it is or I wouldn't be calling," an impatient voice spat.

Fuck. "Hello, Ryan."

"Someone sounds happy to be alive. Look, the next photoshoot is scheduled for the 20th. I just sent you the details. It's editorial for some British fashion magazine so I hope you've been slimming down. None of the foreign clients like beefy dudes." My modeling agent said to me.

"As you have told me probably 100 times before. Didn't I just shoot three days ago?" I asked, poking my soft, beer-filled stomach.

"Yes, you did, but I do not want to hear any crap right now. You should be grateful. The more shoots you have, the more money you have to spend on protein powder and cocaine… or whatever you chose to do in your free time. I'm traveling to Hollywood for the next two weeks because I have boys signing on a new television show, so I won't be easily reached."

"Congratulations," I mumbled.

"I have to go, but call me if you have any questions about the email. I should be around for the next 30 minutes before my plane leaves."

"Okay, talk to you later," I said, but he'd already hung up.

This was the fifth shoot he'd scheduled in the past two weeks. I found the work incredibly draining. I willingly signed up for this life and could technically quit any time, yet there was something about modeling that was intrinsically addicting, like running a race where the finish line is a billboard in Times Square. The first part of the race is perfect, my body feeling good; I'm energized, my knees don't hurt, I'm hydrated and my headphones haven't died yet.

Then I hit about three kilometers and my legs feel like they're dragging through cornstarch. People are starting to pass me, the crowds aren't as enthusiastic as they were at the start and my playlist has hit the weird point where it starts alternating between Lana del Rey and Excision.

The last stretch is not as good as the start but not as bad as the middle; everything still hurts, and although my vision has started to spin, the finish line is the reprieve. Seeing myself on a billboard is exactly like finishing that race.

It's only a part time job, I reminded myself. *I can say no anytime I want.* I opened my email to retrieve the booking information and saw that the studio is two and a half hours away. *Hell no!* I called Ryan immediately.

"I assume you already found something wrong with my generosity?"

"This is two and a half hours away from me. I am not doing that. I don't care what magazine it's for if it will take up a whole day– *and* I have school. This was our deal when I came over here and—"

"That cannot be right. Check again. After the last mix-up, I take extra time to coordinate with your London agents to make sure clients are within an hour radius. When I talked to the photographer, he promised me that you would be able to get to him by bus. Which reminds me, Milan and Paris both want to see you within the next month so I'm working with them to book those flights right now."

"A two-and-a-half-hour bus! I'm sorry but I put the address into Google and it is clearly at least two hours away."

"Oh my God, Landon, I do everything in this relationship," he sighed. "Text him yourself. I gave you all his contact information in the email. Work it out, I know you're a big boy."

"And you get 20% of my total paycheck for what? Sitting around and mooching off the pretty people? You don't work out for two hours a day, monitor what you eat or drag your body to a shoot at four in the morning."

"I get it! God, I will check with him again and get back to you tomorrow. If I don't get back to you beforehand, then you don't have to go. You made yourself clear about your parameters when we first talked about your schedule."

"Thank you," I said more calmly.

"Fine. Talk to you—" But this time I hung up first.

I threw myself back into my bed. Did Sidonie give me the wrong number on purpose or did she just mistype a digit? After staring at the screen for a minute or two, I placed the phone back on my dresser and covered myself in my blankets to watch The Florida Project.

I checked the time. Although I always fast on Sundays during Lent, I was hungry already. Jake told me we ate around 17:30 last night, which means I'd have to wait until after mass before I could order chicken livers from Nando's.

It was only a five-minute walk to Guardian Angels Roman

Catholic Church, but I made it inside mere seconds before the priest called us to stand. Because I was one of the first to receive Communion, I had extra time to reflect on my week. Having been raised Catholic, I never felt that the rules of the Church were morally righteous. They may help keep an orderly society by telling people what to do and how to act, but I'd concluded that I was more spiritual than anything else. My grandmother tells me I'm a heretic, but as I tried to think back on a week's worth of sins, I found my mind wandering to last night.

I could still see her face when I passed her in line, when she accused me of punching her, when I gave her the drink, when she kissed me and when I watched her look at me before she walked away. The more I think about it, the more my heart starts to pound—I felt alive last night. There was no unspoken requirement to continually ask superficial questions to keep the conversation going. I never once felt awkward answering her questions in an honest manner and I knew that she saw me as me the minute I started talking. She was liberating.

God, please, I am praying for one text message. I won't jack off for a week. That's all I need, one message.

I felt slightly guilty about my prayer as I left church, but I couldn't help myself. What was the use of lying to God? He knew the truth anyway.

Nando's had my order prepared when I walked in. I slept with the cashier early in the semester and she'd been texting me ever since. The positive side was that my orders were always on time.

"Hi Melissa," I smiled politely as she handed me the brown paper bag.

"Hey Landon. See you next week."

With someone like Sidonie existing in the world, Melissa may as well not exist at all.

Back in my room, I saw that I'd missed quite a few calls

since leaving. The most recent was from Ryan, so I called him back as I ate my food.

"I do a nice thing for you and you decide to ignore my calls?"

"I was at church," I said dryly.

"I got in touch with Leo and he's only 15 minutes from you. He says you would take the Tube one-stop eastbound to Stratford, then the overground to Hackney Central. He's the street opposite the station."

"What do you mean *he* is the street across from the station? If by he you meant studio, then I'm fine with that. But if you meant 'he' as in apartment, I'm not considering that. I thought I moved onto the big leagues like a year ago, but now I'm back doing creepy apartment shoots?"

"I wouldn't have booked him if I didn't think he was worth your time. He's done a lot of work in the Paris and Milan markets and is just starting to get noticed by some big names. I promise it'll be worth your while, plus your book needs to be updated. Everything you have is too commercial for these markets. He'll add some variety and fresh perspective, which you really need."

"If you say so," I sighed. "I'll be there Tuesday."

"That's a good boy," he said.

"Have a fun time in—" *Click.*

He knew he constantly pissed me off. I guess we both kind of liked the relationship because it made both of us money and neither of us cared about each other. As I placed my phone back on my desk, my heart stopped. The preview of a text message from an unknown number glowed green.

Hey! Remember me?

There was a +33 at the beginning of the contact! I typed "English to French translation" into Google then the words, "The question is, do you remember me?"

La question est, vous souvenez-vous de moi?

Je croyais que tu ne parlais pas français ;)

Shit. I would not be able to keep this up.

Une surprise dans tous les coins, c'est comme ça que j'aime le garder haha... But English is much easier for me.

My chicken livers could wait. All that mattered was this digital conversation. As if she were in my room, I checked myself in the mirror before looking back at the phone.

Waouh for 2 sec i thought you spoke really well French. Sorry I did not text earlier. My phone was stolen last night on my way back to the hotel. I have to use my laptop. Just went back home. How old are you btw?

Bliss filled my chest and radiated outward to my head and limbs. There was a reason she didn't text me sooner. I usually didn't believe someone when they said their phone was broken, but I didn't need much persuading to believe Sidonie. My hands were shaking as I typed my reply.

How old you think I am?

I couldn't believe I never asked her how old she was. Judging by her appearance and conversation alone, I assumed her to be the same age as me. But with everything happening in the States with sexual assault, I would be in big trouble if something went wrong and she was underage.

I would say 21?

I highly doubted anything would have gone wrong, though.

That would be correct. How old are you? Or is that

not something I ask a woman like yourself?

How old do I look?

You acted older than me so for that reason only I would say that you are 23. You don't have to actually tell me how old you are, it doesn't matter to me. And you leave for Paris tonight at 8?

I ate my meal as I watched the three dots hover on the screen. I didn't want to make my obsession too obvious.

I'm 16 years old. Yes tonight around 8pm.

My heart dropped like a stone. *16?* There's no way I was that well-spoken at 16—and what was she doing in a bar, anyway? What was I even thinking? This whole thing was so stupid to begin with. I met this girl who lives on the opposite side of the world. We met once and would never see each other again.

Well now we both know each other's ages that pretty much tells us everything about each other. I hope you have a great time back in Paris!

If I continued the conversation I would self-classify as a pedophile. Emotionally reeling, I started to laugh. It started off as an easy chuckle but five minutes later turned hysterical.

"Bonjour!" Jake said through my gasps as he let himself into my room. "Did you end up going out with that girl today?"

"No, thank God! Dude, she is 16 years old."

"No way!" he laughed, sitting down next to me. "Are you serious? You perv."

"She just told me! I'm telling you, London is turning out to be a weird city."

"I know it."

I shook my head, eager to change the subject. "How was the parade?"

"It was really cool. Wish you could have come out but I could tell you needed a break."

"Well, I got one. Text me tomorrow what your plan is. I know you have the essay for your science class, but even if we just get dinner, I'm down to chill."

"I'll let you know. Seriously, thanks so much for telling me about that... it made my night."

"Glad you're enjoying yourself," I groaned, flopping onto my back.

"Alright, I gotta get home. Talk tomorrow."

"Later," I said, listening as he opened and closed the heavy dormitory door.

I must have drank more than I thought last night. What was it about her that made her so appealing? Turns out it was just another wasted night after all. *No, it wasn't. What am I even saying right now?* Jesus, it was the furthest thing from a wasted night. I got to be myself and she liked it. I didn't tell her anything about modeling, so I didn't have to answer all the bullshit questions I normally got asked. She made me feel something. When she talked, it was apparent that she had thought about her ideas and was not throwing flack at me. I didn't know her but I wanted to—she had everything I was looking for. But it was wrong on so many levels.

There was no way I'd be able to sleep after this. I retrieved some marijuana gummies from my desk and ate double what I normally would, desperate to get her out of my head.

Early the next morning, I felt disoriented. Was yesterday all a dream?

> *I was kidding ;) I really enjoy Saturday night, I hope you tell me if you come to Paris.*

She sent it while I was asleep. I read it over and over again, grinning like an idiot. Shit, I did not drink enough water before I took the gummies. I was definitely still high. I could feel my brain processing information at a slower speed than usual. When high, I also had a tendency to indulge every impulse. Before I even comprehended what I was writing, my finger pressed the send button.

> *I thought you were kidding...when I saw 16 my heart stopped. I also enjoyed Saturday night. I will definitely tell you if I come to Paris but if you do any more traveling let me know too. I am going to Scotland and Norway this coming week, then Berlin and Prague, then Madrid and then Morocco. I also don't know if you like Lana del Rey but if you decide to travel to Madrid between April 19-23, I have tickets to see her and I'm sure she would love to meet you:) have a safe flight back*

Reading my message over, I wished I could redo it. I totally got this trait from my dad; he had no filter when he drank and I guess the same applied to me with weed. Throwing my phone underneath my comforter, I sighed, knowing that I needed to go outside. Victoria Park was right next to Queen Mary so I sauntered out of the building into the damp London air. Mile End had changed so much since I arrived in January. Runners were looping around the neatly paved pathways of the park while families pushing strollers enjoyed the light breeze caressing the skyscraper trees.

I pushed myself too hard at Boston College, which is why I enjoyed London and the other cities in Europe. It was sheer luck that the entire United Kingdom Teacher's Union decided to strike this semester, so by the time I left in June (for hopefully The White House) I would have attended just four weeks of classes over the span of six months. There were no assignments to complete because the teachers refused to grade. I was doing all the work for myself and in the off chance they reached an agreement with the university.

Walking in Victoria Park or taking a stroll through Borough Market were two of my favorite free time activities, but sometimes I got lost in my own head and found myself in Northern England after a two-hour train ride by myself. I didn't know how I got up there half the time, but the spontaneity made me feel alive. Every other part of my day is like going through an infinite emotionless void.

That's why Saint Patrick's Day confused me so much. What was so different about Sidonie? I thought it was the booze, but I'm usually depressed the day after I drink—yet I felt hopeful.

> *i'm turning 22 soon, your plan looks amazing I'm getting jealous, are you in holidays? Im going to Copenhagen in may but I told you that already I think ;) yes I do like her! and I love Madrid but still don't know if I can afford other trips so I let you know*

> *I have a whole apartment in Madrid that is paid for so if you want to do Madrid you'd have your own bed (that sounds so creepy but I am offering the non-creepy invitation haha) But have a good time in Copenhagen and I will keep you updated if I come to Paris again:)*

Walking home, I tried to imagine where she was right now— back in Paris, certainly. Back to her usual life, whatever that entailed. Was she sitting on a balcony looking out at the Eiffel Tower, a view she was accustomed to, as she sipped an espresso after her long trip? Maybe her caramel-colored hair was pulled back onto her slender neck like a real Parisian as she looked down at her phone, reading my messages. Maybe as she did, she was wondering the same things about me.

March 20ᵗʰ

I stopped eating last night around 2000 hours so my body would have more than enough time to get rid of all the excess water I may have stored. This was my normal routine, even though I knew it was unhealthy. Since the beginning of editorial season, especially because London was way less commercial than any United States market, I had to lose about ten pounds since coming to London. It was much easier than I thought because the food was so much cleaner here but there was no excuse for starving myself before a fashion shoot. But here I was, on the Tube at 0800 hours, my stomach groaning loudly.

The journey to the apartment took 15 minutes, just like Ryan said it would, and I was relieved when I got off at Hackney Central. City Mapper told me the apartment was right across the street, and although I had no clue who this guy was, what his pictures looked like or what exactly I was doing here, I trusted Ryan. If he said this photographer was on the rise, I had to jump on that train before it left the station.

As I approached the building, I noticed how depressed the area felt. There was scaffolding everywhere, litter lined the street and the houses were greyer than London. I was extremely out of place in my black skinny jeans and extra-large black pullover—the classic uniform for models.

"Hiya. It's Landon. I'm here to see Leo?" I said into the

microphone after ringing the bell.

I got no response other than the sound of a buzzer. Folding my umbrella, I stepped onto the first floor. As I opened a metal door, there in the first door on my right stood a man dressed in the exact same outfit as me. Everything about him told me he was foreign. His slender face was Italian or French or some sort of Eastern Slavic. His Adriana Lima nose was slightly upturned but strongly pointed beneath slightly bushy eyebrows. His forehead was not a fivehead or a threehead—it was a solid four. His parted lips were heart-shaped, and if he were wearing a different outfit, I would have guessed he got lip injections. The five-o'clock shadow stopped right at his castle-high cheekbones, and his jawline would put Zayn Malik to shame. He had his hair cut the same way as I did—a skin fade with more than three inches on the top. He was barefoot and did not smile at me when I approached, even though I was presenting my usual charming self.

"Ah, I wish you wouldn't do that," he said to me as I shook the rainwater off my umbrella.

"What?" I said, trying to figure out which part he didn't like.

"You're American?"

"I'm Landon. Are you Leo?"

"I am. Come on inside and let's start shooting. I don't have much time today because I have to be at my studio in downtown London to edit some pictures."

I was left staring at where he just stood. *Nice to meet you too.* I was going to tell Ryan exactly how I felt once I get out of here. There was no need for me to put up with people like this anymore—I was trying to move up in my career. That meant demanding respect.

"How are you today, Leo?" I said politely as I stepped inside.

"I'm good. How are you? I got you a cup of water. I know most boys don't like to drink anything else," he said as he set the glass down on the kitchen counter. The place was small but sleek, with modern black finishes.

"I'd actually prefer some whiskey if you have some," I joked.

He looked at me like I was a calf being sent to slaughter, which could only mean one thing; he was gay. *He Is gay. Gay.* There was no question about it. "Are you serious?" he asked. His bangs fell loosely in front of his eyes as he stared at me. The majority of male photographers were gay, and I'd been looked at like this before—but something about Leo was slightly different. *What was it?*

"I'm kidding. Sorry, it must be my American sense of humor," I said.

"That must be the case."

"Is there anywhere you want me to put my jacket, umbrella and shoes, or should I leave them on? I wasn't told anything about what would be going on today, sorry."

He came out of the kitchen carrying two glasses of water, a small Bluetooth speaker, his iPad and a Canon EOS 1D X Mark II. After all these years, I'd actually learned a thing or two. The camera cost $5,000 for the technology and then another $500 for the lens. He must be making some money to have a piece of machinery like that.

"Place your shoes in the hallway. I would rather not have to clean up after you when you leave." He walked past me, not even pretending to look in my direction. What *the fuck* was the matter with this guy?

"Okay." I took off my shoes and jacket and set them on the floor in the hallway, along with my umbrella. "You have a slight accent, are you from London?"

"I am from Italy. The mother country of democracy. I hear you Americans really are into that idea," he said, looking straight at me. His clear ice-blue eyes gleamed as he smiled at me. He was playing a game. This whole act was precisely that—an act. His eyes were too bright to be serious.

"You should know that I don't normally accept models like this. The only reason I accepted you was because your agent reached directly out to me. After I looked you up, you seemed like you had a decent track record."

"Then I owe you a thank you for making an exception. I looked at your work and you are really talented," I lied.

"Oh? Where did you see it?" he asked, placing his camera on the table and fiddling with his computer. This living room was plain as shit, the walls and floors bare. I couldn't believe I was back to shooting in an apartment. Taking a deep breath, I tried to look out the single window in the room, but the scaffolding outside covered the view. *How was he going to shoot with lighting this terrible?*

"I think Ryan sent me a few things," I said.

"I didn't think I sent anything to him," he said quickly.

Actually, I really don't care if he thinks I'm lying. "I don't want to waste your time if you're busy later. Maybe it's best if we just get started...now. Then I can leave."

He took his hand off his computer and peered back at me, his arctic blue eyes finding my soul from a few feet away. Heat rushed to my face. The accent was throwing me off—I loved accents—and he seemed way more composed than he originally let on.

"Actually, would you like to sit down?" he asked. He looked as though he surprised himself, because his left hand slipped off the camera. This was more what I was used to. It was always a red flag when a photographer jumped right into taking pictures without knowing the subject; it showed naivety and inexperience. Finished products always turned out poorly when the photographer did not truly acknowledge the person that he or she was shooting.

"I don't want to waste any of your valuable time." It came out sharper than I intended.

"You won't. Here, put on whatever music you want while we talk." He handed me the iPad.

I typed in my own account on Spotify. Big Wild softly drifted through his speaker.

"I would have pegged you for more of a rap-type American."

"Not for this occasion."

"What occasion would that be?"

"I'm here, aren't I? You are busy. I am busy. We are both busy. I don't want to waste your time and I hope you don't want to waste mine—"

Click. His lens was pointed directly at me and I got the aftershock of a small flash. He brought the camera into his lap and stared at the screen.

"Now I just need to get the light," he said, going back to the table and plugging the camera into the computer. "Sit on that stool over there, would you?"

Disoriented, I mounted the stool. A grey leather couch sat directly opposite me, and stacks of fashion magazines were neatly organized on the coffee table; each one positioned incongruently underneath the one above it to make a spiraling staircase of manicured beauty. The lush tree in the back corner was too shiny to be mistaken as real. Several small frames hung on the back wall, each one containing a photograph of a nude man. There was no supplementary light anywhere in the room, and I wondered what my pictures would look like.

Why couldn't I meet him downtown in a proper studio setting?

Leo was still sitting on the leather couch, laptop perched on the glass coffee table in front of him. I didn't know how much time had passed since someone last spoke - *Where is Absolem?* – and he was too focused to notice that I was analyzing him; he could be a model himself. His graphic t-shirt gripped his lean arms tightly. The Italian accent didn't sound like it had been used in any formal setting in years... maybe it was fake? Was that part of the game too? His focus on the computer highlighted his sharp features, his cheekbones casting a shadow over the lower half of his face.

"I like this," he said suddenly, indicating whatever is on his computer screen. I immediately shifted my gaze to a random picture on the wall.

"Thanks," I mumbled.

He followed my eyes to the picture, mistaking my boredom for intrigue. "That was one of the first men I ever shot. He was a dancer with the Russian ballet and he set a high bar for everyone else. The way he moved in front of the camera made me feel uncomfortable invading his space. It was like he owned the world."

"I can see that."

"Anyway. I like this shot and I know what we are working with. Are you normally this angry?"

The question was so ridiculous that I let out a strangled laugh. "What? I don't see myself as an angry person. I look angry?"

"That's what the picture says. Tell me a little about yourself and then I will tell you my story. I also lied before. I know that you are legitimate, and I don't have to get to a studio later. I wanted to see how you'd react. Sorry, it's a nasty habit of mine."

"Really?" I smirked, now fully intrigued.

"Yes." Our eye contact held for a second longer than I would have liked.

"Uh…" I cleared my throat. "I'm from America, as you guessed. I am a student but I'm over here for the semester. My teachers are all striking right now so I haven't been to class practically the whole time in London, so I've been traveling and writing," I said.

"Where are you from in America?" He pushed all the magazines to the edge of the table to make room for his bare feet.

"New York. Not Manhattan but like an hour outside the

city... from the Poughkeepsie area?"

"Where Vassar and Marist College are?"

"Exactly. You've been?"

"Once, probably five years ago. I went to the States because I was studying finance at the time."

"What happened with that?" I grinned, interested now.

"Your turn isn't over yet."

"Okay then. Well, I'm the oldest of four—"

Click.

"Which tells me absolutely nothing."

"And am studying philosophy and political science along with psychoanalytic studies and international studies."

Click.

"And you are what year?"

"I'm a third year. We call it a junior in the States."

"Then what? What comes next?"

Click.

"I don't really know right now."

"Bullshit. I bet I could guess what you want to do." When his eyes held mine, they were so blue they were almost transparent.

"What would that be? You seem like you have all the answers."

"Politics or some type of business. Not like accounting or finance, but the type of business that forces you to do your job in front of, or for, large groups of people." *Click.*

"That is astute," I chuckled.

"What does that mean?"

"It means keen or clever, like very good at making observations."

"Thank you. You can continue if you wish," he said as he fiddled with his computer.

"I think politics would be cool, but not the type of politics that we live with right now. It's too corrupt. I'm a bit of a hypocrite though because I applied to a position in the White

House this summer, in the office of speechwriting."

"You'd write the president's speeches?"

I have his attention. He's actually listening. "Well, he has a whole team that would write them. Realistically, I would be proofreading them and shit like that. But I think it would be amazing to end up with that opportunity."

"You are interesting. It might be the fact that you are still in academia but you were really tense when you walked in so I thought that you would do business or something."

"I was tense?"

"Your shoulders were close to your ears and you did not look happy to be here," he said.

"I didn't mean to—"

"It's fine. I can tell you about myself but then I want to ask you who your favorite philosopher is."

"Really?" I snorted. No one actually cared about what anybody studied in college, much less a subject like philosophy.

"Is that so surprising?" He seemed taken aback by my pretentious snort.

"It would be great to hear about you though," I said, regaining control. I needed to remain more passive.

"I am originally from Italy. I was just like you. I was studying business and I was always tense. My father was very strict and I spent all my years in Catholic school so I did not have a choice in what I wanted to do later in life. Then my father died—"

"I'm sorry to hear that."

"No, you are not. You did not know my father and you don't even know me. If any of us really cared when someone said that someone else died, we would be crying all day long."

Unsure how to respond, I grabbed my water off the table and took a sip. I really was starving.

"He died when I got a job in finance. That's why I had to go to New York."

"Right."

"When he died, my family drifted apart. It was like he was the thing keeping us all together. But when he died, I knew that I would not be happy in life if I kept doing what I was doing. So I left my country and traveled the world for a year before I came back to London."

"What an incredible story," I said.

"And the best part is that I am not even done." He laughed and took a sip of his water as I placed mine back down. "I traveled all over the world and I found so many happy people and I knew that I wanted to be just like them. Side question, you don't have to answer if you do not feel comfortable, are you gay or straight? You seem like you are straight but you are also a model and most are gay."

"Yeah, of course, I'm straight," I said quickly. We looked at each other for a moment, and his lips parted slightly so I could see his tongue. *His lips are so full.*

"Okay."

"You were saying?" I said, picking my water back up.

"Well, I fell in love with so many people when I traveled the world and it really changed me. I found this beautiful girl in South Africa and she fell in love with me. I spent weeks with her and one day she gave me her father's camera and asked if I could take her pictures. I had no idea what I was doing but I said yes because I liked her a lot. After she got them developed, she told me how good they were and asked me to take some more. Her cousin was an editor of a small magazine in South Africa and she submitted my photos. Anyways, they were accepted and that's when I fell in love with photography. It's the most beautiful art there is because you can capture someone's soul with just one click."

"That is a really beautiful way to put it," I said while he stared at me.

"I thought so. Then I came back to London and started

doing it full time. I haven't been published a lot but I really enjoy to do it, and the best part is that I get to keep falling in love with all different types of people," he said, standing up.

"What an eye-opening story." I followed his lead over to the stool.

"It was for me. I wish everyone could be honest with themselves. It is something I am still working on but at least I am doing so."

"That's good."

"Yes. Before we begin, I do want to hear your favorite philosopher. I bet it is—"

"Kant," we said at the same time.

"Of course!" he laughed.

"What do you like about Kant?" I asked quickly, trying to force the redness out of my cheeks.

"I don't like Kant. I only guessed that you liked him. I like Descartes."

"Cogito ergo sum," I said in my best Italian accent.

"As we all do."

"What made you think I liked Kant so much?"

"Thoughts without content are empty—"

"And intuitions without concepts are blind," I finished. I regretted the playful banter immediately because he quickly diverted his gaze back to his computer. I stiffened.

"I need to say no more," he laughed. "You seem like someone who thinks about a lot of things and is very critical of themselves. You are not like most models I have met. Many are critical of their appearance but not critical of themselves."

"I guess I'm both."

"And how are old are you?" he asked, looking at me out of the corner of his eye.

"I don't see how that fits into the conversation, but I'm 20. I'll turn 21 in a month."

"Really? You seem much older than that."

"Normally people say I look much younger."

"Yes. Yes, you do. But this is all good. Thank you for speaking to me about this. Now, please rearrange yourself on the stool. You don't have to take off your shirt yet because I need to test the light."

"Fine with me." I was relieved that the conversation was over.

"Today," he said as he put the camera in front of his face, moving closer to me, "I need you to do whatever you want. I am not going to give you any direction."

"What?"

He clicked the first real shot. I tried to recover my classic model face, but it was too late—*click*.

"There are no rules. I am taking pictures and I want you to do whatever you want. I have seen your other pictures and they are good but they are too commercial. There are too many rules in commercial modeling which is why I don't sell my soul to these companies and agencies. You are beautiful so I want you to act like you know that."

I rubbed my fingernails together because. This was way outside my comfort zone.

"You said you know philosophy. Do you know about the three ancient Greek figures?" he quipped from behind the lens.

"Uh…"

"That's okay. I will tell you now," he said as he took another picture of my confused and squinting face. He took a step back to look at it and smiled. "I will tell you. There are three poses: the child, the hero, and the god. You are used to acting like the god in pictures because… you are, uh, you are, what do they call you in America?"

"What do you mean?" I asked.

"Someone who plays sports and has a pretty face and has many muscles?"

"A stud?"

Click.

"Yes! Perfect, you read my mind. This is going to be easier than you think. You are a stud in American and studs have many muscles and stand with their hands on their hips like Superman. They always look like they can do anything. You flex all your muscles and don't ever look at the camera because you want people to feel like you do not know they are there."

"Okay?"

"Then there is the hero. You could be a hero but the hero is man. You don't seem like a man. A hero has the same body as a god but he works in different ways. A hero is very fluid, like water, and moves gracefully. It is feminine at its most beautiful point. The hero would sit on this stool and cave in his chest and drop his arms while keeping his hands in interesting positions. Do you understand?"

"Yes?" I looked down at my hands to make sure they fit the criteria. *Click*.

"Yes!" he shouted, skimming over to his computer.

I got up to follow him but he quickly blocked the screen.

"No. You stay where you are. I never show any models my pictures the same day. You should also know that you will only get one or two pictures from me. I spend a lot of time on them—sometimes days."

"That's why they turn out so good," I offered.

He looked up at me and smiled, showing all his teeth in the process. "I know you are lying about seeing my pictures. These pictures you were looking at on the wall are the first pictures you have seen of mine, aren't they?"

"Why would you guess that?" I said nervously.

"You are not a good liar. That is my favorite thing about you so far."

"And the child?" I said, happy to change the subject.

"The child is me. When someone sees me, they think I am in good shape physically but the first thing they notice is that I am skinny. When someone looks at you they don't think you are fat because they are only fixated on your muscles. You are large but your muscles make you not fat. A child is very shrunken and very alone."

He grabbed a picture off the wall and brought it over to me. It was a man with curly black hair. His back was completely towards the camera and the focus of the picture was his protruding spine. He appeared frighteningly thin, but I could see the absolute striking beauty of it. His shoulders were hunched over his legs, not visible in the picture, and I could see the top of his butt. He looked like he was in the process of starting to look back over his shoulder.

"I don't think I can do that. I am also not getting naked," I added sternly.

"I know," he said matter-of-factly.

"You know what? That I could not do the child positions and that I'm not getting naked?" I said rigidly.

"I know both things. I am not asking you to do either. You seem like someone who likes to learn a lot so I wanted to show you what I am talking about," he said, placing the frame back on the wall.

"Good, I just wanted to make sure."

"I want you to start off with god and then make your way to hero. Would you mind taking off your jeans? It will not have the same effect if you have pants on. Plus, by the looks of some of your pictures this does not seem like an unfair request."

He was right, I was used solely for my body. I'd worked on my machine since sixth grade and now was reaping the rewards of the hard work, even if it meant my face was partially photoshopped off an underwear box. I removed my jeans and saw him glance at me as I turned towards him. I can't tell is he was checking me out or if he was looking to see the underwear I was wearing.

"You have another tattoo on your leg?" he questioned.

"I do."

"It's a Celtic shamrock?"

"It is. I got it when I left high school—faith, family, hope and luck. A little corny but it means."

"Means?"

"Yes." I responded.

"I understand, "means". I like it. An unusual way to end a sentence," he said. "Get up from the stool and move in whatever way you want. You can start with the god, like I said, and move from there. I only want to stay here with you for another half an hour."

"Wow! That means a lot," I snapped. Normally I didn't like bullshit and preferred if people told me what they were really thinking. He did that exactly—so why was I being so sensitive?

"Go!" he announced, and I launched into my normal routine.

15 minutes later, the room had changed. He'd switched off my playlist and changed it to something else when I wasn't paying attention. The mood had become audibly more sensual, but so much more relaxing. However, he hadn't said a word since I started, which unnerved me. I preferred constant critique and feedback so I knew what to do. He kept looking at me through that little lens. Feeling directionless, I started to repeat the same positions.

"Go back on the stool. I want to try something," he said at last.

"Is there anything you want me to do before that?" I asked nervously. I just wanted some indication that he was getting imagery that would look good in my portfolio.

"I love them," he said, looking away quickly. I started to bring the stool into the light so the camera would be able to capture my whole silhouette, but he stopped me with his hand.

Photographers get the direct orders of what is expected from a campaign and are required to convey that information to the model. Each company, magazine, or piece of art is intended to have a specific feel to it, convey a meaning. I understood that there was often a necessity for the photographer to touch the model during a shoot, to position them a certain way for the theme. I'd been gripped by the shoulder so harshly that post-production had to remove the finger marks. I'd been manhandled to such an extent that I was sore the next day because the position the photographer put me in was so unnatural. No one had ever moved me so gently as Leo. His hand warmly eased me back down onto the stool. He didn't grip me with his fingers, but guided me with his open palms, heat spreading from under them.

"I don't want you to be in the light. We have gotten too many shots of that. Stay in the dark and remember what that feels like. When I say go, I want you to collapse on yourself but lift you head up to the camera. Use your hands to accentuate your face, cup them on your chest or place them gently on top of one another in your lap. I don't care what you do, but I want curves, not lines. Go!"

I tried to follow his direction, grateful for the guidance. As I pressed my shoulders down and hung my head, my weight shifted so far to the right side that the stool started to slip out from under me. Within milliseconds, a succession of twenty to thirty clicks followed as I completely lost my balance and toppled to the floor. *Never had I been so disarmed that I lost my balance.*

When I stood up, Leo was blushing noticeably. The redness spread from his hands up his arms and disappeared under his shirt, only to reappear on his neck and into his cheeks. He saw me staring and turned back to his computer.

"That was really good. Uh, I think that's it for today. I am excited to look at them. Do you want anything from me in particular?"

"I, uh, no." I stammered.

"Okay. Then I will send your agent these pictures when I

have finished them. They won't be done for a while so don't expect anything soon," he said hastily, looking back down at his camera. "You were…good. Yes, you were good. This was nice."

As I pulled my shirt over my head, I saw one image on his computer screen as he deconstructed his camera. I recognized my body, but that was not me. The person on screen was grace, but I was not graceful. The man in the photo didn't have a straight line anywhere in frame. The definition of every muscle was visible, though I wasn't flexing. My hands were poised on my body as if they controlled the rest of it. It looked nothing like me.

My trance was broken when Leo closed his camera bag. I pulled on my jeans and re-fastened my gold chain.

"It was very nice to meet you. As I said, I will send these pictures to your agent. I understand that you may be used to more professional equipment and a longer time with the photographer, but like I said, I am just starting out." *Was that self-consciousness?*

"You never answered how old you were," I blurted out, immediately paling. *Fuck! Why am I even concerned about that?*

He turned around. "Did you ask?"

"I believe so."

"I'm 28."

"You seem younger."

"You seem older," he said, getting up from his seat on the couch.

"It was a pleasure," I said, sticking my hand out. He looked from it to me and then back to it. I was shaking, but he didn't seem to notice.

"The pleasure was all mine," he said, shaking my hand softly. His sincerity started in his eyes and worked itself all the way down until I felt it in his handshake.

"I'll show myself out," I said, picking up my umbrella and jacket.

He watched me walk out, a simple behavior, but he saw me. Just as I reached for the door handle, his footsteps padded on the wood floor. *One, two, three, four.* He was four feet closer but so far away.

"If you are ever in need of a photographer, just give me a call. Did Ryan give you my number?"

"No," I said, fumbling for my phone in my pocket.

"Here. You. Go," he said as he typed his number into my contacts. "I will send the photos to your—"

"Agent. It might take you a while because you spend a lot of time on them but I will have them soon."

"You listen," he laughed.

"Not all the time."

As I finally left, my hands were hot. I called Ryan the minute I was out the door, but I got his voicemail. On the train back to my dorm, I laid my head on the cold window and replayed the events of the day. I wasn't sure how they made me feel—uncomfortable yet exhilarated. Irritated yet fascinated.

For whatever reason, I hoped to see Leo again.

March 23rd

Hey, this is weird and kind of random but what dates are you going to be in Copenhagen again?

I texted Sidonie the next morning because I had nothing else to do. I had no class, no shoots scheduled for another four days and no museums left to explore. Jake was going to Paris for the weekend to see one of his girlfriends from back home, so I wouldn't have someone forcing me to spend time with other human beings.

As a good student of the world, this extra free time granted me the ability to explore aspects of college life that I'd been too busy for in the States. One of those activities was drinking at a local dive bar near campus called Spoons. Without fail, I always found a handful of my international friends who were down to drink with me.

"Aoife, hiya, how are you?"

Aoife was a northern girl studying English and Drama. She was one of the realest and funniest people I'd ever met. On the first day of Popular Theater and Performance, she called me Ken, as in, Ken—Barbie's husband. She originally let it slip to my face, and the name stuck with all my other classmates. I was Ken because I was the only person, she knew, who looked like they were photoshopped in real life.

"Hi Ken," she said now, matching her stride with mine.

"Where are you off to?" I asked.

"I just got done with some writing for the day. What are you doing?"

"Just having a walk."

"You weirdo. Where are you walking to?"

"Around, you know... I like to wander."

"Right, well, I'm done for the day so if you want to stop being a weirdo and to join me for lunch, then count this as my formal invitation."

"I'll pass. I just ate. But if you want to become a weirdo then you can join me on a walk."

"Fine, if I must," she said dramatically.

"Want to see who else we can recruit?" I enquired mischievously.

"I know Lydia is getting done with class... Joe should also be done. Want me to text them?"

"How about we go find them? Do you know where they'll be coming out of class?"

"I do," she smiled, directing me towards the Bancroft building. We didn't talk as we walked. Even though we met only five months ago, we were comfortable being in silence with one another.

"Lydia!" Aoife yelled into a group of students as a blonde bun turned in our direction.

"Hi guys. What are you up to?" Lydia said, joining our walk.

"Ken wants to go for a walk so I'm going with him."

"I would join you but I desperately need to eat. I haven't had a thing since last night."

"I could eat," I said but immediately wished I could put my foot in my mouth. Aoife looked at me and raised her eyebrow. She knew I desired Lydia, even though she'd been with her boyfriend for six years.

"Ken?" Aoife said. "You must be pretty hungry after all this walking, right? I didn't think you were hungry…"

"If you don't mind, we would love to join you," I said sheepishly. I felt bad that I said no to Aoife and yes to Lydia, but Aoife wasn't bothered by that sort of thing.

"That would be great!" Lydia said. "Joe normally joins me so he should be out in just a minute. We could do a group lunch at Spoons or something?"

"I will not be drinking," I said quickly.

"Oh, there he is!" Lydia wrapped her arm around Joe's waist, and he kissed the top of her head. He wasn't the boyfriend but, they could be in another world. Aoife grinned mockingly at me.

The three Brits walked just ahead of me, as they always did, chatting happily. The idea of community was so different over here compared to America. In Boston, community was pretending to listen to someone at a party then forgetting what they said as soon as you walked away. Here, everyone was so intertwined. Joe, Lydia and Aoife all genuinely loved each other. Granted, I got incredibly lucky to have them as friends—not everyone was this open in London. A lot of the other Boston College students had kept to themselves since coming abroad.

"Landon, what have you been up to, mate? We missed you on Saint Patrick's Day," Joe said, noticing I was taking a back seat to the conversation.

"I'm sorry about that, guys. Jake and I got a bit sidetracked and we ended up meeting some kids from BC at a bar in Chinatown."

"If you say you went to Waxy O'Connor's, I will roundhouse kick your ass right here, right now," Aoife threatened, but I was already smiling.

"Of course he went there, classic American," Lydia said.

"Did you have a good time?" Joe asked.

"The place was disgusting, but I had a good time. I met a girl from Paris I thought was really cute. We talked all night and—"

"Then you took her home," Aoife said sharply. "We know the deal."

"I did not end up taking her home, which is one of the reasons I'm so obsessed with her right now."

"Key words *right now*," Aoife scoffed.

"Find someone else then. There are enough hens here that would be honored to spend a night with you," Lydia mocked.

"I doubt that's true."

"You know you're Mr. Hot American to the girls here. They all know what you do."

"There is so much more than being told I'm hot. Would I be hot if I didn't model?" I asked, trying to start a philosophical conversation.

This time Aoife kicked me. "Stupid question. Now, let's get drunk."

Even though I said I wasn't going to drink, four glasses of wine arrived at our table courtesy of my classmates. The three of them downed their glasses while I sipped on mine. We didn't even have our food yet when another round arrived at the table. I lied when I told Aoife I had eaten earlier, so by the end of my second glass I got the feeling around my eyes telling me that I would indeed be getting drunk this afternoon.

"So, Mr. Model, have you had any shoots recently? Lydia and I saw you in a storefront in Central London the other day and the cashier, for some reason, did not give us a discount when we said you were our brother," Aoife said.

"Maybe because I'm not your brother?"

"That's not what we told the clerk." Lydia looked at Aoife as both of them burst into a fit of laughter.

"Come on Aoife, let him be. It must be so difficult to be so attractive. Think of how hard it is to take off your shirt and have someone take pictures of you," Joe smirked, and the girls laughed harder.

"It's not funny!" I said, but their laughter made me chuckle.

"I'm serious though, have you had any—" Aoife began, but my phone rang and interrupted her train of thought.

"Give me one second. I don't know who this is," I said, squinting at my phone.

"Mate, let it go to voicemail," Joe said.

"What if it's important?" I said, standing up.

"What if it's an employer and they want to conduct an interview?" Lydia said.

"I'll buy the next round if that is the case. Give me one second." I moved away from the table on wobbly legs. "Landon North."

"Landon?"

"That's me. Who is this?"

"I'm disappointed you don't remember me."

"If you tell me who this is then maybe your chances will get a bit better," I said, and for some reason my voice got more seductive. There was a pause on the other end. "Who is this calling?"

"It's Leo."

I got immediate cottonmouth. "Ah, well you should have said that earlier."

"Is everything okay? You seem a little bit off."

"Why wouldn't it be?" I said nervously as I burped up alcohol gas.

"Have you been drinking?" he laughed into the phone. "It's like one o'clock!"

"Slightly– but that, for your information, is none of your business. What's up?"

"I just wanted to tell you that I have the pictures all done."

"Really? That was much faster than I would have thought. How did you get my number? I don't remember texting you."

"Yes, well after you left I thought that I had gave you my home phone number instead of my cell phone. I called Ryan and asked for your number so I could correct the mistake. Unless I did type my number in correctly and you just didn't text me."

"Nope, you may have given me the wrong number because there was no caller ID when I picked this up."

"Then I guess I made the right choice," he said.

"I guess you did." *Did I miss something? Was I supposed to have contacted him for something?* "Is there anything else?"

"Ah, right, I wanted to tell you the pictures were done."

"I bet they look amazing. I can't wait to see them. Are you going to send them to me or Ryan? Ryan is out in Hollywood for a while so I might need to give you my email so I can have them first. He never gives me anything until like a month later anyways."

"I was actually wondering if you wanted to go over the pictures together?"

"Together?" I said into the phone. The wine made it seem like a statement, but it was definitely a question.

"I don't normally work this way with models but when I feel really passionate about something I like to make sure both sides are happy with the final product. I was thinking if you're free this week, we could pick a time for review. I took over a thousand photos but have narrowed them down to 100 and would like you to tell me which ones you like the best."

"You want to go over the pictures you already took?" I re-iterated to make sure the booze was not mixing the message

"Yes, only if you want to. If you don't prefer to work this way that is fine with me but I wanted to give you the option."

I felt heat seep into the tips of my ears. "Look Leo..."

"Before you respond, I wanted to let you know that this is not what you are probably thinking this is. You said you are straight so I am not asking you out over the phone, it's just that...the pictures turned out really great and I think you will be very impressed with them. It is what Ryan wanted for you."

I'd be reminisced if I said I had not thought about the final picture I had seen on his computer. The vulnerability of the half-naked body and the dark background, sitting on a single stool with nothing else around me—it was a sight I had never seen before. Leo was able to capture that moment unlike the many photographers who came before him.

"Give me one second," I said.

"I'm not asking you out, I—"

"I'm checking my calendar."

"Oh."

The phone screen was a little blurry, but there was absolutely nothing to do this weekend. It would be beneficial to see the pictures before Ryan. He never sent me the full folder because he thought I would somehow find the time to redistribute every single one of them, therefore exhausting the surprise for the bookers and casting directors.

"How does tomorrow sound? I know that's a little short notice but I have a clear weekend. I like to save Sundays for my own personal outing or whatever."

"Now it sounds like you are asking me out on a date," Leo laughed.

"Don't get ahead of yourself."

"Tomorrow works perfectly for me. Want to meet for dinner?"

"I thought you said it isn't a date," I said quickly.

"I did not know that eating food automatically meant a date. You Americans must be dating everyone."

I stifled a laugh. "Dinner is fine with me. I was just testing you."

"It will be professional. One of my friends is the owner of a very nice place in Central London so I will ask him if we can have a table."

"Text me where I should meet you and what the dress code is like. I'll see you tomorrow at whatever time works best."

"We have many things to look at and I hope that you are, what Americans say, on your A-game, because I have brushed up on my philosophy since we last talked."

"Have you now? Then I guess we'll have to see who comes out on top." I said, regretting my word choice immediately.

"To the victor belong the spoils," he said.

"You've brushed up on American history as well. I'm impressed."

"See you tomorrow then. Don't drink too much more wine; I'm not sure Ryan would like that."

"Screw Ryan," I mumbled.

Leo laughed. "Goodbye."

I wiped my damp palms on the front of my jeans. Maybe I was overthinking things. Maybe he really did just want to go over the photos. But if I wasn't sure, why did I say yes?

My friends were watching me curiously from our table, their faces flushed from the alcohol. Aoife made a kissy face, and I gave her a swift middle finger, which caused the rest to laugh.

"Who was it?" Lydia asked.

"My agent," I lied.

There was a nervous and excited fluttering in my chest that I couldn't shake, and it didn't seem to be caused by Lydia or Sidonie or any other beautiful girl. It must be the wine.

March 24th

I wanted to follow up because I know how creepy that last message was. I didn't mean that I was going to follow you there. I know you probably think I am a weirdo and I promise that I won't text you again. I hope you have fun in Europe.

I knew it was a mistake to text Sidonie yesterday. How pathetic that I resorted to sending two messages over the course of two days with no response. Although I never was one for one-night stands, despite what people may have thought, adolescence basically functions like a string of them. Try out this personality. Don't like it? Try this one. Like it but still not perfect? That's okay, take a piece of it and then try out that one.

I would be lying if I said I knew who I am or who I want to be. However, I recognized I was closer to achieving that goal compared to others, simply because of my innate privilege. Traveling the world, and seeing sights billions would never have the time or resources to witness, helped with this self discovery. I attended schools that brilliantly marketed themselves as institutions where the greatest minds shape their dreams so that, one day, those dreams would become reality. My parents—the authoritarian superstructure who melded machine with human flesh—made us into something greater than life. The North dynasty would rise above the clouds even when the world was falling to the depths of hell.

I was grown to become a charismatic businessman, charmed to meet everyone I should encounter. Kindness alone wasn't enough—I wanted everyone I met to fall in love with me. The only thing lacking from this perfect life was consistency; my parents said consistency was settling and settling was boring. Consistency was like trying to drive through traffic. Never in my life had I experienced that phenomenon; I woke up early to beat everyone to work, accomplished a lot then came home late. I missed traffic every step of the way.

My neighbors, classmates and friends would argue that my life was exciting and entertaining. They said that their lives were dull and uneventful in comparison. Yet each night they went home to people who have been there, supporting them, since the beginning. They had driven through the traffic with people who they knew would ride with them until the end.

I would argue that conversations had on car rides are equally as fulfilling as reaching the destination.

Nevertheless, I was a driver. My feet were planted solidly on the gas pedal, so much so that I forgot where the brake was. Sure, the emergency brake was right by the shifter, but I had only ever pulled the emergency brake once. My eyes were radars, spotting every open opportunity and weak point in traffic patterns. I exploited reaction times of slow drivers while out-performing the other drivers who had shittier cars—privilege had placed me in the front seat of a Ferrari. My "trucker radio" was more like a synthesizer; it took my words and reoriented them so I was relatable and desirable. I was the wizard behind the curtain.

There is something rewarding about discerning your actions in spite of reason. I sometimes complained about the lack of substantial relationship in my life—the type you can "go home to" at the end of the day—yet I placed myself into situations that limited the possibility of constructing a future with someone. One of the reasons I sent texts to a girl I will never see again was so I could entertain myself until something else, a distraction, came along.

That connection was not, and could not, have been real with Sidonie. How could it? People cannot make that much of an impact on you in such a short time. I won't text her again.

I already cherished the amnesty that tonight would offer me because this night was still all about me and there were no expectations. I let the possibility wash over me as I finally rolled out of bed. After I hung up with Leo yesterday and walked back into Spoons, Aoife, Lydia and Joe could see something had changed. The conversation instantly became oriented around topics of substance. It was as if they sensed a change. We talked the pursuit of happiness, the concept of tradition and fulfillment. We cycled through each one of these topics just as quickly as I cycle through my own life but there was something different as we reached the third, fourth and fifth glasses of wine. We grew together to momentarily step over the defense mechanisms we had self-constructed. As Lydia and Aoife started happy crying by the end of the afternoon, it was a representation of human nature in its most pure form. It was why London was home.

My meeting with Leo was scheduled for 1900 hours at a quaint restaurant in Central London. Leo was correct in his assumption that I preferred something "un-American" to eat. After I worked out, I researched the restaurant and was impressed. Chef Jacques DeChambolé was a fascinating character and unbelievable artist. His track record was littered with exclusive dinner parties and celebrity caterings. His restaurant, Blanchette, was among the most elite and renowned restaurants in all of London. The thought of dining in a place of that caliber sent tingles up my spine.

Leo sent me all this information after I had sobered up and he made a clear point to say that I should dress in whatever I felt most comfortable in. The emphasis of this particular point made me nervous. Paranoid thoughts swirled in my mind as I tried to figure out if we would actually be attending dinner at this exclusive place or if I had made a grave mistake in trusting someone I'd only met once. Many photographers and directors had attempted to trick me into dates in the past, but Leo seemed different.

"Hi," I said to the hostess as I arrived. I glanced around to make sure my level of fanciness matched everyone else's. It seemed I had the right idea in my sport coat and slacks, but I somehow didn't fit the part like everyone else.

Refraining from acknowledging me, she held up one finger as if she were on the phone, which she wasn't. I waited another five minutes before speaking again.

"Hello."

"Do you have a reservation?" she said sternly, still not looking up.

"I believe so."

"Name."

"It is under Leo Morreti." I chirped.

This time her head snapped up. "I am so sorry, Mr. North. Please let me take your coat and I will bring you to your table in just one moment." She blushed as she stripped my coat from my shoulders. "I am so sorry about that…it has just been busy tonight and I did not expect…"

"It's quite alright," I said quickly, alarmed at her reaction. "I can do this by myself, thank you though."

"No. No, Chef has been waiting for you. I'm here to make your time at Blanchette as comfortable as possible. Can I get you something to drink or a glass of water?"

"Uh, no. I'm fine, I'm sure there will be water when I sit down."

"Then please let me bring you to your table." Turning on her heel, she led me through the restaurant.

It was early but the place was already packed. Now, noticeably underdressed, the heat swelled in my cheeks as I made my way through the dining room. The walls were powder blue and appeared to be made out of velvet. There was a single rose in the middle of every table, and the plates and cutlery were adorned with elaborate paintings. The ceiling was that of an old-world cathedral; gold flakes reflected the dim light, making the ambiance even more sultry. Ornate paintings adorned the walls. There was no one my age in sight, and everyone I passed seemed surprised to see me.

"Excuse me. Is Leo already here or am I the first to arrive?"

"No, sir. Leo arrived just over an hour ago. He and Chef have been conversing for quite a while now."

"I'm not late, am I?"

"Of course not. Leo said you would be here right on time."

We approached the last available table in the restaurant, and although it was empty, the woman did not slow down. "Just this way, please." She gestured towards a thick leather door, and my stomach dropped. Leo rented out the private dining room. I knew it. This really was just all a ploy to get me to go out with him. *How could I have been so stupid?*

"If you just follow the sous chef's station around the back, you will see Mr. Moretti waiting for you. If there is anything else I can do for you, please let one of the chefs know and I will come back as quickly as I can."

Instead of another dimly-lit private dining room, I was greeted with the clashing of dishes and an overpowering flood of white light. I was eating in the kitchen.

"Thank you," I managed. I followed the nearest metallic chef station around to the back, and there, situated in a roomy corner was Leo, seated across from a man who was noticeably in command. I watched their interaction. Every few seconds, a different chef came over to the older gentleman, who tasted what they'd cooked and made a variety of different faces.

The lesser chefs then scampered off in search of whatever was needed, and he and Leo picked up the conversation wherever they left off, not missing a beat.

I was way out of my league here. Not only would I be interrupting the conversation but I was the youngest person in the entire restaurant. No one should take me seriously.

"Mr. Moretti, I presume?" I said when I was finally within earshot of the table.

The whole kitchen paused as if they had been waiting for me to speak. *I am in Ratatouille.* I half expected the kitchen to erupt in song, but just as quickly as they stopped, they resumed.

"Landon." Leo exclaimed.

"Leo, this is just amazing," I muttered as I shook his hand.

"Let me introduce you to one of my oldest friends and the man of the evening, Chef DeChambolé." Leo gestured to the outrageously tall man standing next to him. I'm almost six feet two inches tall, and I had to crane my neck to look the man in his eyes.

"Leo, mon vieil ami, tu es trop gentil," he said to his friend before directing his attention to me. "You must be the friend I have heard so much about."

"Really?" I raised my eyebrows at Leo.

"Not really. I kid," the chef said dramatically, and the two laughed. "This must be a special occasion because I rarely let anyone use my office as a dinner table."

"It is much too kind of you to let us sit here. Your restaurant is absolutely beautiful. I can't imagine what the food must be like."

"Thank you for your kind words, it is my pleasure," he said in a thick French accent. "It seems that my time for old friends is up. Let me bring you two men something to start with and then we shall make you the very best of France."

"Thank you, Chef," Leo said. "So how do you like it? I want to reiterate that no matter how badly you want this to be a date, this is not a date. I knew I couldn't have asked for a table in that stuffy old dining room." Leo smiled, and the unspoken tension evaporated. "Don't tell Chef I said that!"

"You could have not picked a better table. As long as the food is good, I'll be happy. How did you know I like French? This cuisine is very much a hit or miss type of food."

"You like philosophy. I think that says enough," he said as he brought his laptop out of a bag under the table.

I peered through the beautiful chaos of the five-star kitchen. People were yelling at each other in dialects undecipherable to me, and food was flying in saucepans and pots like a hurricane.

"I met Chef when I first came to London. We were both at a party together and one of my friends introduced us. I had just broken up with my girlfriend—"

"What?" I laughed. I was so embarrassed that my hand flew to my mouth, which only made the situation more awkward.

"Does that surprise you?" he asked calmly.

"No. I just thought—"

"It did surprise you. You thought I am gay, yes?"

I hesitated as he eyed me down. "If we're being honest," I said slowly.

"Should there be any other way we should be communicating with each other?"

"Excuse me?" I said, shaking my head.

"You said 'If we are being honest' and now I am asking you if we should communicate in any other way. Your statement would imply that you were not being honest with me before."

At first glance his face was void of emotion, but his eyes gave him away. He didn't look hurt, but somewhat disoriented, as if what I said had knocked him back, like a blow to the chest.

"I didn't mean I wasn't being honest. You're right, I had an assumption about you, but I was by no means acting on that until you either confirmed or denied it."

"Interesting that you say that. I also made assumptions

when I first met you."

"And it seems that you still are."

"Because you have confirmed or denied nothing for me to replace those assumptions with. This does not matter! I'm sure we will visit this again at some time. I want to show you some pictures before Chef comes back with whatever he is preparing," he said, opening his laptop decisively.

The kitchen was even louder now, frantic cooks rushing past us on every side. Leo seemed completely content in this setting. Finally, just as I saw DeChamborlé turn a station carrying a pot of mussels, the first picture of the series loaded. I knew it had been edited because there wasn't a single blemish on my face, but it wasn't the lack of imperfections that captivated me; the picture displayed on the screen was not an accurate representation of me. My face took up the entirety of the screen with just a marginal trim around the edges, making the background colors visible to highlight my skin.

There was nothing I could think of to say. I was so used to criticizing myself or the photographer, but this, sitting here with Leo, was a completely passive process. I absorbed everything. In the photo, my head was downcast but my eyes were panning up as if to look directly into the camera—except that was not the case. I tried to look into my own eyes, unnaturally vivid on the screen, but it was impossible. There was a small shadow cast on my neck, and my collarbone and tendons had been emphasized. My five o'clock shadow had not been scrubbed, and the focus was so clear that I could see every individual piece of hair protruding from my cheeks and chin. I tried to slide forward in my seat to look into my eyes again, but I couldn't meet them—there was no way to change what had already happened. *I could not connect with myself.* Finally, I saw what Leo had said during the shoot—I looked angry.

"It's beautiful, is it not?" he asked.

I didn't have time to respond because Chef was placing a

steaming plate of snails and mussels down on the small table.

"Masseurs, tonight I have specially made escargot stuffed with truffle butter, garlic cloves, parsley and shallots. It is one of the most famous dishes here because no other restaurant in London knows my secret ingredient that I use. Hint, it has to do with vodka and white wine. Then, I had Acel prepare you mussels with cream, wine, butter and parsley. They are two of my favorites but also the simplest. When you eat the mussels, I have found that it is best to inhale as you do so. This way you get to taste all the flavors in your nose as you swallow. So many of these people have no idea how to eat. They just shove everything in their mouths like Americans—"

Leo cleared his throat.

"Ah, yes. I apologize for that. Not all Americans. Forgive me, I was just trying to give you the best way to eat."

"Thank you," I said, watching as Leo moved his laptop to make room on the table.

"Would you two prefer to pick the rest of your meals tonight, or shall I?" But it was not a question at all; we wouldn't have the option to look at a menu if we wanted to.

"We will leave it up to you, Chef. Neither of us are in any hurry, I don't think?" Leo said, and I nodded. Chef bowed slightly before disappearing into the turmoil of the kitchen.

"Do you like it?" Leo asked as he grabbed the first mussel from the pot.

"It's amazing. It looks nothing like me."

On screen now was the same exact picture but from a further distance. The collarbones and the stool legs were the only straight lines in the whole picture. My head was titled towards my chest as if I had fallen asleep mid-picture. This time I had to clear my throat before I responded. The picture was closing in on me.

"It's beautiful."

"Then tonight was not a waste after all."

"I didn't think it would be."

"Then I will scroll through a few more and you tell me which ones you like the best so I can start building an album of them. I was hoping to send them to Paris for an exhibit. Would that be okay?"

"Yes," I whispered, then made myself louder and repeated the word. I'd seen thousands of pictures of myself in the past three years—what made these so special?

"I'm waiting to show you my favorite until the end." He put the plate of escargot in front of me.

Over the course of several hours we looked at hundreds of pictures. The only way he could have edited this many pictures was if he worked nonstop since I saw him last. We didn't talk much as we looked, and it unnerved me a bit, but the food was too good to stop eating. Chef made us duck with cherries, steak tartare and a cheese and bread soup, and we devoured more French pastries than I thought was possible. There were six glasses of wine, expertly paired – three for me and three for him, each of different varieties, but not enough that I felt drunk.

"Now before we go. I want to show you my favorites," Leo said just as my phone vibrated in my pocket.

"Let me just answer this message. No one normally texts me this late."

Yeah you made a mistake in texting me that six days after we spoke.

My heart dropped right out of my chest.

"That's okay. I need to use the toilet anyway," Leo said, but I didn't acknowledge that I heard him because my heart was frantically beating at Sidonie's message.

I know, I'm really sorry again.

I had to spend all last night talking to the people at the hostel trying to add a room for our trip.

Her immediate reply startled me.

Funny!

I am not laughing. You owe me $40.76 for three nights. I accept Venmo, direct deposit, wire transfer, etc.

I looked at the picture message underneath her last text message and saw a screenshot of a receipt with my name on it.

Wait, I am having a hard time figuring out if this is real or not.

It's real. You had better book your flights or train soon though because prices are going up. If you don't find me on Venmo then I will request you. Don't try excuse of school work because you do not have any classes.

okay?

We have the room April 13 – April 16th*. I will see you then!*

See you then? I typed, still unsure if this was a joke or not.

Not if you don't book your flight soon enough you won't.

"I hope I didn't keep you waiting," Leo said as he sat back down.

"Not at all," I said, stuffing my phone into my pocket.

"Is everything okay?"

"Oh yes, fine."

My heart was pounding. Sidonie wanted to see me? I wrung my hands as the photo loaded on Leo's laptop. As the image came into focus, they stopped mid-squeeze. There is no spoken language that can describe what was before me. In the image, my body was water. *Did he liquefy the picture?* I was mid-jump like a ballet dancer, which I most definitely was not. My toes were pointed directly at the floor, arms outstretched in either direction, my head perpendicular to the lens of the camera. My whole silhouette was shrouded in a brilliant warm glow. Every single muscle and tendon was beautifully positioned. My hands were curved neatly into themselves and looked far more feminine than I had ever seen myself, but they didn't look out of place or unnatural.

"I call this Hermes," Leo said.

"Hermes?"

"You capture flight in such an effortless way. Look how both of your feet are equidistant from the ground and are both pointed in the same intensity. If I added wings to them, it would look like you could be flying along a pathway in the sky."

"Hermes," I repeated. Another Greek reference.

The pictures that followed were even more brilliant than Hermes. I couldn't understand how not a single other person in my life had been able to capture me like this. This stranger completely transformed how I look at myself. Shouldn't all photographers, or many, be able to produce similar images? But they weren't.

In total, there were 20 more pictures after Hermes. The night was drawing to a close, and I found myself wishing it could go on. The kitchen had calmed down since we first entered—I wondered what time it was.

"Gentlemen, can I assume that you have enjoyed your meal?" Chef asked with a smile.

"It exceeded all expectations," I said.

"You are welcome back here anytime. A friend of Leo's is a friend of mine. I mean that."

He said something to Leo in French, who only smiled and shook his head. Chef DeChamborlé shook my hand before he walked away, and on que, the hostess came in to give us our jackets. Silently, Leo and I dressed ourselves and left through the service door of the kitchen. The night was much colder than I would have expected, and I braced my shoulders against the wind.

"Are you going to take a taxi back to your home?" Leo asked. He didn't seem cold.

"I'm going to take the Tube."

"I will walk you there then."

We walked in silence for some time before I said, "We never talked philosophy."

"I was hoping we could save that for another time," he said, stopping to look at me.

He looked so relaxed. The air was brisk but I felt everything around me. The latest glass of wine couldn't be the culprit because we had spent four and a half hours in the restaurant and the booze was poured according to the course.

"I think that would be a good idea," I said as I glanced into the station. No one was coming in and no one was coming out. We were completely alone in London.

"Should I call you or would you like to call me this time? Now that you have my correct number, I'll know it's you when you call. I can always call you if you like though. I know you must be busy." He looked incredibly young as he spoke, his cheeks flushed from the cold. This moment was not what I expected—it was beautiful but not like his pictures. The moment was beautiful because it was untouched. The flickering light from the station changed how his face looked every second or so. There was an instant where he looked like he just woke up from a long nap in the sun, then another where he was tired and full of anguish.

Suddenly it was like I was looking down on the scene from above. Both bodies—one shorter and lean and one taller and muscular—were frozen. They were standing just two feet from each other and the air around them was encompassed in a glittering sheen. The artery was pounding on the right side of Leo's neck. The heat coming from the underground station was refracting the light, almost as if it were a spotlight in some Broadway play, casting it directly onto the two people onstage.

The moment started moving again and the muscular body took a single step forward while the lean body stayed put. By the time I was catapulted back into my body, it was too late. Whatever I wanted to be doing in this moment didn't matter; it was out of my hands. I was already fully leaning into the space between us. I placed my hands on either side of Leo's neck. He leaned into me and our lips touched.

Adrenaline surged through my veins and I was stripped of everything that had ever encompassed my identity. I was not kissing another man, another man was not kissing me. In fact, nothing was happening. There was just energy transferring from one life to another with absolutely no boundary. I never imagined that I would be in this position, but in this moment, I couldn't imagine going another day without it. After just a couple of seconds I broke away and was jolted out of the trance-like state.

"Then I guess we have a date," Leo said.

"Uh…" I struggled, the heart rising to my face.

"Thank you for joining me tonight. I had a rad time, as you Americans say. I hope to hear from you soon?" Leo said, looking away. The gesture was out of respect for me so I did not have to recover any words or look him straight on. He understood.

"That's more Californian. I'm from New York."

"What?"

"Californians say rad. I'm from New England so if we're

going to have another night, you should know that New En-glanders say 'sick' or 'wicked'."

"I will remember that."

Just like that, the night was over in a split second. And just like the night, my life had diverted down a path that was barricaded for so long. I was in my dorm before I even real-ized that I boarded the Tube. I was showered and staring at the ceiling of my 80 square-foot dorm room before I knew what had happened but when I thought about the moment, it felt like something that could be happening right now or in a hundred years. The timeless nature scared me. *How long will I remember this?* He didn't touch my face when we kissed even though I touched his. Was I too forceful or was it not custom-ary to put your hands on someone for something as simple as a kiss? *What am I even saying?*

I'd been caught in an elliptical orbit for my entire life, but I just got hit with a comet and now I was somewhere I had never been. It was so different but exactly the same. There were beautiful shapes and colors on both sides but one was illuminated and the other was not. If anybody were around they would have surely thought awkwardly about our inter-action. On one side you had a boy, noticeably younger than the other, gently caressing another man's face while that man stood like a statue with his hands at his side.

More time passed and I realized I was brushing my teeth in the mirror. My reflection hadn't changed. Did I expect it to? Everything appeared exactly as I left it, but I knew that from this moment forward, I would look back on my life in two parts; the me that existed before this night, and the me that existed after.

April in London: Part 1

April compounded March. The Copenhagen trip with Sidonie was constantly on my mind but I wasn't nervous. *Why should I be?* Sidonie went out of her way to change her plans to accommodate me. I felt bad thinking about it, but if she was willing to go that far, then how much work did I really need to invest when I was there? This single narcissistic thought turned over again and again in my mind, but soon her innocent smile entered back into my headspace and I quickly changed my tune. I went from being calm to incredibly nervous. *She changed her plans for me.* What were her friends going to think? Didn't she say she was going with friends? I was going to be the odd one out.

How was she going to introduce me? She would have to make something up because no one would be stupid enough to invite a person they'd met once at a bar in London for a spring break trip. Didn't this happen in movies? A girl unknowingly invites a charming sociopath on a trip and then he goes on a rampage. *She shouldn't have trusted him.* That's what her friends would all say. Of course, I wasn't going to kill her. But what was I going to do when they were all speaking in French together?

These thoughts consumed me as my semester abroad ended. I had finished every final exam—which would never be graded but legally had to occur—and now had even more free time. Every free moment I spent thinking about Sidonie, her sapphire eyes and that laugh I'd only heard for six hours during a single night out. When I wasn't thinking about or talking to Sidonie, I spent my time with Leo.

I was hesitant to see him after the last date because I couldn't understand how I saw my new self, much less how his view of me would change. These thoughts vanished when I finally did see him again. I felt obligated to call him for the second date because he had obviously put in effort for the first. Four days after the restaurant, he picked up on the second ring, saying, "This is sick, bro." I laughed. He laughed. The laughing lasted for three minutes. Me in my dorm room. Him in his apartment. There were no boundaries or social ques that either of us followed because, for some reason, neither of us thought to pay attention to them.

The second time we saw each other was more ordinary than the first. There were no pictures to review and no fancy table in a five-star kitchen; we met in Hyde Park. I thought it was cliché, meeting in Hyde Park, because it seemed to be too romantic for two people who had no idea what they were doing. I thought he was going to laugh at me when I suggested it but that moment never came. All he said was, "Should I bring my camera? There are a lot of cool things at night that you can't see during the day."

We planned to meet at the exit of Knightsbridge station, fully aware that there are multiple exits to Knightsbridge. He said it would add to the adventure and it did. That evening, we ended up walking in circles because my phone didn't work without Wi-Fi. I had gone the entire semester planning ahead and using City Mapper to find my way around. Finally, as I was about to give up and go back down in the station to ask someone for their phone, I ran into him; I literally ran into him. He was coming up the stairs as I was coming down. His bag fell to the floor and he started cursing in Italian until he realized it was me who knocked it out of his hand.

We sat on the floor of the station laughing like two dear drunk friends. I guess we were friends, but we were not drunk. As he inspected his camera, I profusely apologized, but he confirmed that it had not a single scratch on it. I also noticed that he had four bags of scones and three jars of clotted cream and jam in the bag.

As we ascended the steps, he took my hand in his. I was so shocked that I recoiled. I stopped on the stairs, took a deep breath, then took his hand and continued walking. I could do this. For some reason, I needed to do this.

I attempted to ask him about work, the weather and his weekend—which works on every other human being in the entire world as a way to generate small talk—but quickly realized that I needed to change my game if this was to go somewhere. *Do I want this to go somewhere?*

I tried thinking of some deep philosophical topic but was distracted by the sheer number of homeless people, or rough sleepers. I saw them under piles of blankets on the side of the road, begging for change on every corner in London, and still never paid them any heed. But apparently in Hyde Park, nighttime was their playground. Hyde Park was clean of suits, dresses and designer dogs and replaced with groups of rough sleepers seated on benches, lying on the ground in sleeping bags or huddled near the various structures erected in the park.

"I'm so sorry Leo. I didn't realize it would be like this at night."

"Don't apologize, I think you picked an incredible place to spend an evening. This is what I was hoping for." He let go of my hand and gave me a swift kiss on the cheek, igniting a fire in me that turned my skin bright red. *It was wrong for another man to kiss you.* It didn't matter that it was only on the cheek. The whole thing was not biologically correct;

the Catholic Church had told me that much. Leo either didn't notice my reaction or didn't mind; he asked me to get the jam from his bag.

"Hungry?" I asked as I searched for the jam.

"It's not for us. We're going to make some friends tonight. Trust me, I love doing this."

He walked toward the pond, leaving me sitting alone. He marched over to the nearest group of rough sleepers in his sport coat, trousers, shined shoes and gelled hair, sitting down beside them without a word. I watched him from a distance and began to hear the words of caution my parents had given me before I came to London: "Landon, don't stay out too late. Landon, London is not safe at night. Always travel with a Brit when you go out. There are neighborhoods in London where people get shot—be careful."

Leo beckoned me to him. *Shit*. As I approached the group of eight homeless men and women, I realized that Leo knew these people. He had already opened the first bag of scones, which was being passed around the circle, and he had withdrawn a knife for the jam and cream.

"I want to introduce you all to my new friend Landon. Landon wanted to come here tonight because he heard about all that happens at Hyde Park... at dusk," Leo said mischievously as everyone smirked.

Most of them had already begun scarfing down the scones but a few who had not yet received the jam and cream stuck out their hands to greet me.

"I'm Charlie. It's nice to meet you, Landon. We haven't seen Leo in ages, but we're all so happy that he brought a friend tonight."

After the handshake, I wiped my hand on my jeans without meaning to. *Shit*. Charlie didn't seem to notice, and neither did anyone else it seemed—except Leo. He offered me a sad smile.

After the others finished introducing themselves, I stared

stupidly at Leo. I imagined I looked just like my second dog, Macy. Her head cocked to one side, her ears perked up and she stayed like that with her tongue out. I felt like I had been given a command I didn't understand. Leo was too busy having a side conversation with Mary to notice that I was looking at him. Thank God he didn't see me spying because if he saw the emotion in my eyes, he would be able to hold my heart in his hands forever.

"You going to open the jam and cream or are you going to keep it for yourself?" Lizzie asked. I looked down at the two jars I was cradling in my left arm.

"Oh my gosh, no, of course, here you go. Please, take as much as you like. I believe Leo has the knives."

"Your friend is so good to us. We all thought he moved. So much has gone on since we saw you last, Leo!"

The troop had completely finished the jars of jam and cream and sat licking their lips and fingers for a good 20 minutes. I was accustomed to speech about politics, money, family and the future so when my new friends started talking about topics like food and heat, I sat there completely baffled; I was unable to offer any of the rehearsed words of wisdom that had been engrained in my mind by normal societal discourse. They each told me their life story; where they came from, what their life was like growing up, what they wanted their future to look like when they were young, where they went wrong, and why they were not just looking for handouts but were looking for help. They must have thought I was mute because I only sat there nodding.

"I am afraid Landon and I have to go soon. I need to see a few other friends before the night is over," Leo said after an hour had passed.

"We love you Leo. Thank you for coming to see us tonight. If you need us to point you in the right direction of anyone, we know who's in here tonight," Lizzie said.

"Thank you. I want to go see Ed, but Landon and I need to stretch our legs anyway—I'm sure we'll find him somewhere."

I stood up and prepared to march onward. I felt like a wanna-be do-gooder, nothing but a fraud.

"Would you mind…" Leo began hesitantly. The group of eight all nodded eagerly, ready to help their friend.

Leo snapped a multitude of pictures of the nine of us. They did not pose, but simply sat talking to each other as they split the final scone into very small pieces. Leo finally put his camera down, and I quickly looked away. I didn't want him to know how I'd been staring at him, even if he was taking my picture.

The group all thanked me for coming and told me to come back if I ever needed anyone to talk to—they were offering me support. As Leo and I walked on into the darkness, my eyes felt hot and wet.

"There are only a few more people I need to see," he said.

"Okay," I said quietly, not wanting my voice to give away the fact that I had a lump the size of a tennis ball in my throat.

"I do want to apologize. I know this is not what you probably expected, but since we first talked, I started reading scripture again to reorient myself. Your tattoo reminded me of how blessed and fortunate I am."

I looked at the ground. "I don't know what to say."

I saw fear coat his entire face as he brought his hand to his head. "Mi dispiace molto. Sapevo che avrei dovuto farlo da solo!"

"I have no idea what you said. But this is the best night I have had since I got here."

His eyebrows raised. "This is?"

"I thought we agreed that we wouldn't lie to each other."

Leo smiled. "If you liked them, you should meet Ed. He will curse at you until he gets his own jar of jam. I always bring one especially for him."

I extended my hand in the darkness, inviting Leo to take it.

He laced his warm fingers through mine, and I embraced the tingle of fear that mixed with the joy as we walked on.

Jake started to notice that something had changed when I started turning down our customary Donut Time dates, our Monday evening tradition. I told him I was never around because I had "too much work." This excuse held up for about two weeks, but then I accidentally let it slip that the change in my mood was due to the fact that I'd finished all my finals and had no more class. He called me out on it and I quickly tried to backtrack—that didn't mean that I didn't have work. Then I changed my answer again, saying that the internship search had come to a halt and I hadn't received any offers... which was a lie. It was the first time I'd ever lied to my best friend. The internship excuse held for another two weeks and then I changed it to some other bullshit.

The afternoon or evening dates with Leo quickly turned into all-day adventures. When I wasn't working or wandering, we took trips and explored England together. I was nervous to go with him and I didn't understand how I could be more confused than I had been before. *This should be figured out by now.* I was becoming more emotionally attached to him and was beginning to feel something that I hadn't felt in almost six years.

At the same time, I was in an online relationship with a girl I was going to see in Copenhagen. The conversations with Sidonie turned from superficial text messages to night-long phone calls. Neither Sidonie nor Leo knew anything about each other, and that was how I was going to keep it until I could figure out how to pick between them. *Though, I am not dating Leo. I can only date Sidonie.* Surely there would come a day when the choice would be obvious? I made pros and cons list to speed up the process. It did not work. I seriously imagined what it would be like if I didn't have one of them in my life. That didn't work either. One of the greatest confusions arose when I realized that neither relationship had a physical aspect to it. This had never happened before. Most relationships I had been in were because of the physical component. If I thought someone was attractive, I slept with them—it was simple.

My dates with Leo were just dates. I never returned to his apartment and he never came back with me. He had tried to, but I told him I wasn't ready for that. It pissed me off because although he only asked twice, both times after telling him, he said that he understood. He understood? *What the fuck does that mean?* I never understand when people told me no. This man was so wise that he did? Did he think he was special or something? Or was he playing a game with me, knowing that I became more and more attracted to him each time he said he "understood?" How can someone respect someone even when that other person is not getting anything they want? I didn't understand it.

On the other hand, Sidonie told me every time we talked how excited she was to see me. I responded with the same words, but that was all it was—words.

The semester reached its final two weeks and I had gone on a total of eight dates with Leo. The week before I left to see Sidonie was when he asked for my summer plans and if I was returning to the States. I quickly shut him down, not only because I did not want to lie to him, but because I didn't want to think about the possibility that I would choose him and still have to go home. Sure, I got excited when we talked philosophy or when he would make a joke that only was funny in Italian, but the whole male-on-male thing was not what was intended of me. How could I entertain that possibility without the comparison of Sidonie? When he asked me what jobs I might have, I said that I didn't know. He quickly realized that the topic was not open for conversation. He tried to make a plan for the weekend of April 14th but I deflected and said I'd already planned a trip to Copenhagen to see a few friends.

By April, I was somewhat sure that I desperately needed Leo in my life, but I didn't know how I needed him; each time we were together, I always wanted more. I was honest with myself in that I knew I was attracted to him. There was no logical way I could deny that. Unfortunately for me, that realization was solidified before I went to Copenhagen. It was on a day-long trip to Brighton. I wanted to get another tattoo by one the famous artists working at one of the shops down south. I had spent a month designing it and knew exactly what I wanted and where I wanted to put it. I had originally planned the excursion with Jake, but Leo said we could make a beach day out of it.

We took the two-hour train to Brighton, but when we got there, I was alerted that my appointment was canceled because the artist had to attend to a family emergency. I was ready to explode.

"I just came all the way down here from London. I put down a deposit and I won't be in England for much longer. I had this appointment scheduled for over two months!"

"We are sorry, sir. We will happily give you back your money as well as a discount on the next appointment. We know it's not ideal but Mike just received the phone call this morning and had to leave immediately," the receptionist said.

I turned to Leo to back me up, although that was the most illogical thing I could have asked for. He smiled at me and then spoke directly over me to the receptionist.

"I am so sorry. He's a little cranky today. He has been looking forward to Mike's work for a while now and is just upset. I will go feed him and he will call later to schedule a new appointment." He grabbed me by the shoulders and escorted me out the front of the shop.

"Are you fucking kidding me?" I said the minute we passed through the open door.

"Do you hear yourself right now? You're blaming someone

for something that they have no control over," he laughed.

"We took the train all the way down here—"

"And now we will find something to do. Come on, it's 21 degrees and there are beaches we can use. We'll get some lunch and I'll buy a bottle of wine and towels."

I huffed in his direction and stomped onward. We got lunch at a beautiful café right on the water and he told me to meet him on the beach. After I collected my things, I went to find him. I didn't think England reached temperatures over 65 degrees Fahrenheit, but here I was, basking in the sunshine.

By that point, Leo had seen me shirtless too many times to count, as I agreed to be his muse so he could submit my pictures to some galleries in Milan and Paris. When he left lunch to find a spot on the beach, he told me to look for a pink bathing suit, another one of his strange requests. I didn't see how he could guarantee he could find a pink bathing suit on such short notice. With my feet firmly planted in the sand, grains rising between my toes as I walked towards the water, I kept my eyes peeled for pink. All of England was taking advantage of the weather today and the beach was swamped. However, there was not one pink bathing suit in the entire sea of people. Maybe I was going the wrong way. I changed my direction and started down towards the other end. Then I saw it.

A flash of neon pink caught my attention down by the water and I squinted through the glare. My stomach flipped and that is when the realization dawned; I couldn't believe I'd never seen him shirtless before. There he was, emerging from the water, pink bathing suit sucked comfortably against his body. He was running his hands through his hair to keep it out of his face and everybody was looking at him. *Oh shit.* My heart pumped violently, injecting blood into every part of my body. *He's ripped?* He had absolutely no fat, but was not rail thin either. *Why did I imagine him as rail thin?* The tattoos on his arms glistened as the water beaded off his olive skin.

That's what I'd always wanted to look like—did I want to be Leo or be with him? It seemed so easy for everyone else to figure this stuff out—they know they like men, so they seek men, or vice versa. Why was I still so confused?

His muscles rested tightly underneath his skin; it looked like I could bounce a quarter off him. He had a clear six-pack, and his obliques ran down the sides of his hips in the perfect 'V'. I didn't have a 'V' like that. Here I was assuming I was more built than Leo all this time, when it was obvious he went to the gym almost every day. *He never brought that up, once. Not once. I probably seemed like such an asshole.* I was about to turn around and pretend I didn't see him when he spotted me and waved me over. I took a deep breath. What was I getting myself into here?

We sat in the sand together and I relished the warmth of the sun on my face, keeping my eyes closed so I didn't have to wrestle with the desire that came with seeing Leo like this. He fell asleep a few minutes later after drinking a glass of Riesling, and I couldn't help but stare.

I kissed him goodbye swiftly when we arrived back in London, both of us exhausted and dehydrated. I could feel the sunburn developing on my shoulders with each passing hour.

"Bye," I said, turning to go. "I'll miss you."

It was the simple truth—I said it without even thinking about it. I missed him anytime I left, to be honest, even when I was texting Sidonie. Leo seemed as caught off guard by the statement as I was. He stopped to look at me with some seriousness, and my heart sank. I shouldn't have said that.

He stepped forward and kissed me then more deeply than he ever had. My muscles tensed as my mind resisted the reality of making out with a man. But as the seconds passed, my mouth softened against his, and soon my whole body went limp, giving into the sweetness of the moment. I pressed myself against him and allowed myself to enjoy one of the best kisses of my life.

Suddenly, the idea of going home and packing for Copenhagen filled me with dread. I didn't want to leave—I wanted to be here with Leo.

"Enjoy your trip," he said with a smile.

As I looked at his clear blue eyes, I doubted that would be possible.

April in Copenhagen

Copenhagen seemed to me what the world would look like if there was no more war, poverty or violence. It was clean, the people were respectful and you could hear someone sneeze from the airport.

But then I started to think... it was almost too clean, the people too respectful and the sneezing almost too perfect. I had fond memories of my last trip, just over a month ago, and when I landed this time the realization dawned on me that nothing had changed except me. Everyone still had blonde hair, blue eyes and beautiful smiles—and they avoided Americans like the plague.

Sidonie sent me the directions to the hostel as the plane touched down, and I was grateful that the group wasn't going out of their way to meet me at the airport. I was the outsider on this trip and I wanted to make it clear that I knew my place. I couldn't imagine her friend group as people who were mean or cynical, but I also knew not to make assumptions. I urged her to tell me which of her friends would be coming but she never gave anything up. I could hear the excitement in her voice when she would shut me down, saying, "It'll be a surprise. I thought you were down for anything."

This unsettled me because how could I prepare the charm if I did not know the type of people to prepare it for? I wanted her to tell me everything we would be doing, but at the same time, I loved that I wasn't in complete control. For weeks Sidonie and I had talked about everything that could be talked about over the phone, and over the last couple of days, our conversation had begun to dwindle. Simply being together was the only way to see if there was any type of relationship to be had going forward.

After getting my bag off the trolley, I rode the metro-rail right into the heart of the city. I purposely did not tell Francine, my friend who lived there, I was coming back because this trip seemed special. I wasn't going to post anything on social media and hadn't told anyone, except Jake and Leo, I was returning. It was my attempt at keeping these four days a secret, something I could have just for myself. I assured myself that the odds of running into her were so slim that it was stupid to even worry about it. This was about me and Sidonie. This was about finally knowing the truth about myself.

I arrived at Copenhagen Central Station and looked up the address she had given me. It was only a five-minute walk to the hostel. I nervously collected my bag and set off in search of the lodging. At the conclusion of those five minutes, I looked around me and laughed. She had given me the wrong address on purpose. I peered up at the massive five-star hotel in front of me. We could never afford to stay here—I was only paying $40 for three nights.

I dialed her number.

"Hello?"

"Funny joke," I said. "Can I have the real address now please?"

"What? Is everything okay?"

"Just send me the address and I'll be right over to meet you."

"Landon." This time her voice sounded different.

"Yes?" I pushed my ear into the phone to hear her better.

"Landon!"

I turned around. Walking out of Hotel D'Angleterre in a blue sundress was the most carefree, beautiful girl I'd ever seen. She moved effortlessly, and people were watching her from inside the hotel. The doorman didn't even open the door for a couple arriving because he was fixated on Sidonie.

"Welcome," she grinned.

"I was expecting a hostel. I paid for a hostel, didn't I?"

"I did a little photoshopping on the image I sent you. You actually paid for one of my dinners." She laughed, placing a hand on my arm.

She took one more step forward, and something came over me. I dropped my bag to the sidewalk and she threw herself into my arms. She smelled exactly like she did at the bar—a mix of some expensive perfume and butterflies. I'd never had the chance to smell a butterfly, yet I knew this was what I smelled. It was as if I were on acid. The world melted away and a body-shuddering peace settled over me. Without asking myself what I was doing, I kissed her, inhaling her presence. She expected it, because she leaned into the kiss so deeply that our teeth grazed each other. I'd met this girl just once, but it felt like we'd been together for decades.

My arms wrapped around her waist and I couldn't let her go. *This is too good.* I'd harshly judged couples who showed this much affection in public because I always thought it was fake, like they were trying to convince themselves they loved each other. Now I took that all back.

I slowly let her down, trying to remember every part of her that I just touched. The slits in the side of her dress left her bare skin open for me to feel, smooth and warm like her lips.

"Bonjour madame. What a pleasure it is to see you," I said in my heaviest accent.

"Bonjour monsieur, le plaisir est tout à moi."

"I heard something sounding similar to 'pleasure' in that,

am I on the right track?" I beamed at her.

"You would be correct. We cannot be late. I waited here for you but we're meeting the others in just a few minutes. Come put your things in the room and then we must go."

Our PDA did not go unnoticed. The entire street around us seemed to stop and was staring. Luckily, the doorman had recovered and graciously opened the door for us as we walked into the foyer of the hotel.

"How should I pay you for this? I was not expecting this at all."

"You don't need to. My parents are paying for this whole trip, and I assume you have stayed somewhere this nice before."

"And why would you assume that?"

"You seem like you have done *this* before."

The insinuation confused me. I tried to make eye contact with her but she pulled away and looked toward the elevators.

"We must hurry because the water is not going to stay cold forever."

My room was immaculate, with no bags to be seen. It smelled like fresh sheets and lavender.

"Who am I staying with?" I asked, hoping she would say herself.

"You can party all you want in here."

"Where are you staying?"

"That is none of your business. Drop your stuff and let's go get a cab," she said merrily.

"You never answered my question."

"Maybe I will answer it later," she winked.

Sidonie led me by the hand back out into the sunshine, her fingers small and cool in mine. As she hailed a cab, I stared at her baby pink fingernails. We were holding hands as if we were a seasoned couple. It felt normal. It felt amazing. I focused on this feeling, made a note of it in my soul so I would know it forever.

The cab ride was silent, void of unnecessary banter. There was no need for words—they were too silly and small to articulate any of this, anyway. This was peace like I'd never known. I breathed her in and basked in it.

As the cab driver slowed down, Sidonie reached for her wallet. I beat her to it, shoving a 100 DKK at the driver.

"I have to start repaying the tab I owe you," I said. Sidonie rolled her eyes, but she was smiling.

I stepped out of the cab and found myself standing in front of a restaurant called La Banchina. But didn't she say something about water?

"Sidonie, par ici."

I squinted into the sun to see Hercules walking towards us along the wooden dock. The people laying on their towels under the warming sun raised their heads as he passed. He was 6'4" and all muscle. He definitely wasn't a model—his gait was too masculine.

"That's my competition?" I asked, trying to be lighthearted. Did she bring me here to show me that she can do better? He can talk to her in French, and if I've learned anything, it's that communication is a fundamental aspect to any relationship.

"That's only if you think you haven't already won," she said before skipping towards the guy. She threw herself at him and he caught her in mid-air. But there was something different about their embrace. He didn't wrap his arms around her or spin her around; he just let her dangle from around his neck. Once she was back on her feet, she motioned for me to join them and I saw them exchange a brief word as I got closer. He raised his eyebrows at her and she laughed but shook her head. The man was even more massive as I get closer.

"Landon, I would like you to meet Victor. Victor, this is Landon."

I put out my hand to shake his, but he dapped me up instead. I thought that was an American thing.

"Pleasure to meet you," I said.

He was silent and looked cold as stone. My heart sank.

"Victor?" Sidonie said nervously.

His deathly stare broke then and he burst into laughter.

"I am just messing you! We are pleased to have you here with us. She has told us so much about you. Come, we are just about to go into the water." His accent was much thicker than Sidonie's.

I laughed halfheartedly. "Oh, okay."

He led us down the dock towards the remaining tribe of friends; eight of them, all paired up into couples. As we approached, I was reminded of several years ago when I was watching Twilight with my sisters. At the beginning of the movie the audience is introduced to a gorgeous band of foster-children—the Cullens. There was a slow-motion shot of the Cullens walking into the cafeteria, each completely absorbed in their significant other, ignoring the entire environment around them, while Anna Kendrick gives a brief backstory of each of the couples.

Sidonie was my Anna Kendrick as she told me who was dating who. It was easy to decipher between each couple as they clung to one another, each stunningly beautiful. *The most insane coupling I had seen in my entire life.* And that's when I realized—this was a couple's trip, and I was with Sidonie. Could it be?

"Victor is one of my closest friends," she added at last.

"He's very handsome. Do you ever—"

"No. I was just kidding about my comment, Landon. Do not be worried. I only told them good things about you."

Seated in front of me, but beginning to stand, were four men and four women. They all appeared older than me. The men introduced themselves politely; Victor, Ethan, Martin and Axel. The women each gave me a kiss on each cheek; Adrienne, Chloe, Noelle and Valerie. Was this heaven?

After the introductions, each of them paired back up and lustfully reattached themselves to each other. The women were all wearing soft sundresses, and the men were constantly adjusting their hands as if trying to worship every conceivable inch of skin beneath the fabric.

"D'accord, tout le monde est-il prêt à intervenir?" Axel murmured between planting kisses on Adrienne. He didn't even look at the rest of the group when he spoke.

"Axel, English please," Sidonie said as she linked her arm with mine. Everyone's eyes gravitated toward me, sizing me up, casting away their first impressions now that there was some kind of sign that I was invited here for a reason.

"I forgot," he said.

"Good idea though," Sidonie said brightly. "Who else is ready to get in?"

"Let's do it," Ethan said, running his hands up Noelle's shiny bronze legs. She took the hint, lifting her dress up over her head to reveal a red bikini.

"We're going to jump in there?" I asked Sidonie as quietly as I could as the group stripped down.

"Are you scared? Maybe you want to pay another 100 DKK and take a cab back to the hotel?"

I joined the group, stripping down. Axel caught my eye and winked at me, saying something to Chloe.

Sidonie grinned. "He said your body is a work of art."

"Bullshit," I laughed.

"And Chloe agrees," she added before plunging into freezing water.

I followed, and the minute I hit the water I was transported to another planet. It was not only colder than I imagined but also much clearer. As all the breath was sucked out of me, I saw Sidonie's outline a few feet away and swam towards it. She waited there, tempting me to come for her. I pulled her feet and she sunk beneath the surface to meet me. The water was unnaturally clear and both of us had our eyes opened. Her friends were already swimming back towards the dock to get warm, but we stayed.

Heat rushed from deep storage and warmed my fingers, ears, lips and underneath my eyes. I stared at her, her image blurred like watercolor. I pulled her into me and kissed her. *I love you,* I thought as her mouth melted against mine underwater. *I love you.* It was simple.

When we surfaced for air, something had changed. She smiled at me and turned to swim back to the dock. *I can't possibly love her.* I knew the thought would gnaw at me for the rest of the trip but, knowing myself, rationality would take its hold and I'd be placed back where I started.

After we dried off, I discovered that Sidonie was the trip organizer. While everyone else ogled over their significant other, Sidonie was the one keeping us on track. No wonder I was attracted to her. I must have seen something like this in her when I first met her. After the polar plunge, we wrapped our towels around us and walked 200 yards to an old stone building. I felt the heat before I saw the steam—a sauna. The ten of us had the heat to ourselves and even though everybody kept forgetting about the English-speaking rule, Sidonie was right there translating the conversation for me.

It surprised me with how vulnerable her group of friends were with each other. Although they were not speaking directly to me, the conversation veered towards substantial topics: love, mostly, but also family and future. They covered the same topics that I originally talked about with Sidonie, yet I was struck by the complexity of the conversation. I had said much less to Sidonie than I had thought. She was happy taking a back seat from the conversation, laughing when someone said something stupid or funny, sobering up when they said something profound. She was a woman that required very little, and I hadn't had that in my life for a very long time.

"Hey," I said quietly.

"Hi."

"Thank you for inviting me."

"Thank you for letting me know that you wanted to come."

"The text wasn't too creepy?"

"If it was too creepy, I wouldn't have let you come."

After a half-hour in the sauna, we got dressed and made our way to the glass markets in the main town. I had been here with Francine, but I pushed that out of my mind and tried to experience it as if for the first time. Sidonie and I split from the group and found ourselves in a sea of food and drinks. The two glass buildings that encompassed the glass market were filled with tourists and locals, all speaking to each other in a blissful way. Here, time was not linear.

After lunch, we rented bikes and rode around until we got to Christiania. Christiania was unlike every other legal weed-selling city in Europe. It was a series of cardboard shacks and buildings with a massive amount of marijuana in each of them. Just like the glass markets, we split up and all bought our own strains. Sidonie and I got Pineapple Haze. We smoked right then and there.

The four days passed quickly. Weirdly enough, on one of the nights we went out, I saw Frankie, the girl I went out on a date the last time I was here. She immediately understood what was going on when I saw her, and she smiled at me.

"Landon!" She strode over to me in the middle of trivia night.

The French glared daggers at her, but she seemed completely unfazed.

"Frankie!" I said nervously as she gave me a kiss on the cheek.

"I'm so happy you're back in Copenhagen! What are you doing here?"

"I decided to come back with a few of my friends. Can I introduce you to Sidonie?"

"Yes, please! Wow, you are so beautiful, Sidonie."

"You are too. Landon didn't tell me he had friends in Copenhagen. How do you know each other?" Sidonie asked.

So we went on one date. It was before I ever even met Sidonie. What was I so worried about? She dated people before she met me, too, though I didn't want to think about it. That's life.

"Oh goodness, I know Landon because he studied in London. I live in Saint Albans, which is right outside of London, and I know one of his good friends, Francine, really well," she said confidently. She caught my eye and I smiled gratefully. It wasn't technically a lie.

"That's so nice. It's funny that you ran into each other," Sidonie said, putting her hand on mine. Frankie noticed and took it as her que to leave.

"Well, I just wanted to say hello. It's always so good to see you," she said.

"It's so good to see you," I agreed.

"Bye—"

"Oh Frankie, wait! I have to tell you that I took your advice from our last conversation," I said.

Her eyes lit up with curiosity. "About what?"

"I ended up watching one of the movies you told me about, *Call Me By Your Name*? It was you who told me about that, wasn't it?"

Her whole demeanor softened, "Wasn't it just wonderful?" she paused, looking directly in my eyes, "I, I knew you'd like it."

"It was."

Frankie bent to kiss me on the cheek before returning to her table.

"She is so beautiful," Sidonie said quietly.

"But you are even more," I said, kissing her on the lips.

We won trivia that night and walked home ahead of the rest of the group, shrouded in the cool night breeze. My head was swimming from the cocktails and it dawned on me that I had never felt so happy in my whole life.

When we reached my room, she followed me inside without question. I locked the door and wrapped both arms around her waist, pulling her against me.

"Can I stay here with you?" she whispered.

My heart fluttered. It felt like a middle school crush, the storm of infatuation brand new and shockingly vivid, the only thing that existed.

"Yes."

We flopped onto the bed and she burrowed her head against my chest. We laid in silence for a few minutes before she slipped her hands underneath the sleeves of my t-shirt and dragged her fingernails along my biceps. I shuddered. The moon in the window cast a blue-white sheen on her exposed legs.

We slept together that night and every night after that. It was the best sex I'd ever had. When it came time to go, I invited her to Madrid for my birthday the following week. She booked her flight then and there.

"I'll miss you," I whispered into her hair as I hugged her goodbye. Then I remembered saying the same thing to Leo four days earlier. I meant it with him, and I meant it now with Sidonie.

"I hope you will," she said.

I dragged my suitcase through the airport, completely alone for the first time in days, and finally stopped to listen to the noise of my consciousness. Surely it would reveal something important.

Instead, all I heard was what I already knew: *I love her.*

April in London: Part 2

I laughed into the phone as I trudged through the busy airport. "I didn't take off all my clothes! We kept our underwear on."

I was a fraud.

"That is crazy," Leo laughed.

"It was crazy but so much fun! Afterwards we went to this really old sauna and sat in there for an hour until someone finally said they were getting dizzy. Then we did the whole glass market excursions, but we spent the weekend mostly just chilling out. It was so nice to be off work and everything."

"Who are these people again? You never talk about any of your friends."

"It doesn't really even matter. I've known them for some time now." A lump hardened in my throat. What would happen if I told him the truth?

"I'm glad you had a fun time. I'm even more glad that you called me when you landed. I missed you, bro."

"You think you're clever?" I grinned. "I would work on your American catchphrases." He paused, and I could hear him breathing on the other end of the line. "Leo, that was a joke. I don't want you to think that I don't find you clever. You have mastered American slang in my eyes."

"No, it's not that," he said, and his voice tightened. "It's just good to talk to you."

Nervous butterflies rose in my stomach. Why would someone get choked up after not talking to me for just four days? It made me anxious—I shouldn't be allowing any of this to happen.

"I, uh, have to get on the Tube. Want me to call you tomorrow and we can do something?" I said as I tapped my Oyster card to the terminal.

"Tomorrow?"

"Yes. Does that work? I'm going to lose Wi-Fi any second."

"What about tonight?" he said sadly, and his tone made me think about the possibility. I knew I wasn't being fair to him, but no one said he had to continue this relationship with me if he wanted to have sex. I was standing in the middle of five o'clock rush hour traffic and people were watching me lug my bags through the narrow passageways.

"I don't know about tonight."

"Four days is a long time to spend away from you."

"I just have to get back to my dorm and put all my things away."

He paused before conceding, and the nervous energy that consumed me melted away. I didn't know exactly what he wanted. I didn't know exactly what I wanted.

I clutched the phone to my chest in the middle of the London Liverpool Street Underground entrance. People were giving me dirty looks as they passed me; some were even going out of their way to bump into me to tell me to get a move on. The tears welled behind my eyes before I knew what was happening, and a police officer broke away from his partner to approach me. Even as he walked in my direction, I didn't move my feet. The tears continued to build until the first one dripped down my cheek.

"Oy, mate. You okay?" he said as he sized me up.

"Yes, I'm sorry officer," I said as more tears started to run down my cheeks. They were the only sign that I was actually crying. My breathing was not altered, and my body felt relaxed.

"You need to get going. You're blocking the exit for the other passengers."

"Yes, sir. Sorry about that," I said as I walked towards the elevator for the Central Line.

I looked at the elevator bringing so many people up from the underground, none of them paying any attention to me. None of them knowing a thing about my silly, tiny life. Each one of them—the little kids, the busy moms, the lonely old men and every strung-out, overworked and madly in love adolescent and beyond—each had their own distinct set of stressors on their minds. My life was totally inconsequential, just one more in a vast sea of them. One more young man confused about his sexuality, one more self-centered kid being reckless with other people's hearts. I fell in and out of love too easily, too fast. If any of these people knew my story, knew why I was crying, they would scoff at me.

Before I reached the bottom, a little girl in a bright blue tutu and leotard caught my attention. With a small purse over her shoulder, she must have just come from dance practice. Her mom walked behind her, carrying a large duffel bag and talking on the phone. As our positions evolved—mine getting lower, hers getting higher—we stared at each other. She waved at me, smiling. Unable to move my arms, I just stared back at her. I followed her gaze until she got even higher, and then I turned all the way around in my place, looking directly up. As she was about to step off the escalator, she put her little hands together and shaped them into a heart for me.

"Eh, mate, turn back around. We have to get off here," the man behind me said gruffly.

"Sorry," I muttered.

I spent the duration of the commute back to my dorm looking at myself in the plastic windows of the train. People were packed like sardines on these trains, which gave me ample time to think about the innocence and unadulterated kindness of that little girl. The scary thing is we were all like that at one point in our life. It felt innocent and pure to hold Sidonie in bed each morning, just like it felt right kissing Leo in Brighton on that sunny day. It was liberating to feel that which could not be wholly understood. It felt right to cry.

How could I ever decide between Sidonie and Leo? As I considered a future with each of them, it struck me that neither could provide a sustainable relationship. I would never stay with either of them once I got back to the States this summer. What would happen to the time spent here? What would happen to this surplus of love I felt?

Shockingly, my dorm room was exactly how I left it. Despite the fact that years seemed to have passed, that I had transformed completely, my small bed and weathered dresser remained.

As I unpacked in silence, Jake called me.

"Hey," I answered.

"Welcome back."

"Thank you, sir. How have you been?"

"I had a great time in Amsterdam with Andrew and those guys this weekend. The real question is, how was Copenhagen? I cannot believe you flew all the way there to meet up with the girl from Saint Patrick's Day. Was it worth it?"

"I cannot even begin to describe what the weekend was like, dude. I definitely would rate it as one of my best trips yet," I said.

"I want all the details when I see you. Look, I know you're probably tired, but I wanted to make you aware that the internship decisions came out for the White House about 20 minutes ago."

My heart dropped. I checked my email 20 minutes ago and there were no new messages. "No way. How did you turn out?"

"That's actually what I'm calling about. I got the President Economic Advisory Council."

My heart sunk even further. I had no doubt he would get it. He was in the Honors Program of one of the top-five undergraduate business schools in the entire country, and on top of that, he was brilliant. He told me he spent an hour and half talking with his interviewer, and right before he hung up, our President literally got on the line with him. I should be happy for him, but it was my dream to get that internship. If I didn't receive a position in the Office of Speechwriting, I would be crushed.

"Dude, I knew you would get it. If anyone deserves it, it's you," I said halfheartedly, but he was too excited to notice my lack of enthusiasm.

"Thank you so much, dude! I know we talked about rooming this summer so if you get it, I'll put a deposit down for a connecting room or something. How much fun would that be?"

"Without a doubt. Let me check right now if I got anything." I opened my laptop and saw that my inbox had a single message in it. It was a message from the White House. I took a deep breath and closed my eyes as my mouse moved over the message. I clicked on it, eyes still closed, and after another deep breath I opened one eye.

Dear Landon: We are pleased to inform you that you have been accepted for a position in the Office of Speechwriting for the President of the United States.

My hands were shaking over the keyboard. This was one of those moments that had the trajectory to change everything for me. Not only would I have an internship this summer, but I would basically be an automatic shoe-in for any open positions on Capitol Hill come senior year. I strangled a joyful yelp because I remembered that Jake was still on the phone. If I told him I got it I would practically be committing to the unpaid internship right then and there. He would put down a deposit on housing tonight. I would have no choice but to follow through with that commitment. Then came an even stronger reality: Sidonie and Leo have both talked to me about my plans for this summer. They both said that they might be leaving London and Paris respectively, depending on what opportunities come up, but they would most likely both try to be in Paris—Leo for his photography and Sidonie for her art procurement job.

"Dude, I don't have anything yet," I said. *Liar.*

"Ah, really? I was sure you'd have gotten it after they waitlisted you last year. But hey, maybe they haven't sent out all the acceptances yet. The director said notifications begin on April 17th and that not all acceptances would be out by then."

"If I get it I'll call you right away and we'll start planning for this summer, 100%."

"I knew you would say that! Want to do Wednesday night Donut Time before you head to Madrid?"

"Yes," I said quickly. I was tired of lying, but it would buy me more time—time that I desperately needed.

The next morning, I worked out for the first time in four days. It brought me peace to know that blood was still flowing into my muscles. I always got anxious when I didn't work out for an extended period of time, and it didn't help that my agents were constantly asking me for updated digitals. This was the longest expanse of time I'd gone without a shoot since I'd been in London. I didn't have anyone telling me I was too fat, too muscular, too masculine, too feminine, too commercial or too conventional.

At home, I sat and stared for some time at the email from the White House. A few weeks ago, I thought that was all I wanted. But now that it was mine, I wasn't so sure. How did these institutions expect a young person to give up their summer so they can then talk about the "non-bullshit" role they played inside that very company, only to sell their soul to a new corporation the next summer? That didn't sound like a life to me.

Society prides itself on its ability to outsmart every other species on the planet. We pride ourselves on our dominating and manipulative qualities that allow us to subject the earth to our will, but we're doing it to each other in the process. I had a hard time believing that every single young person in college wanted to work at a desk and make money. I didn't know what I wanted, but I knew it wasn't that. Still, I wanted to make money so I could provide for my family, the way my parents were able to financially provide for me.

With time to kill before I needed to meet Leo, I reverted back to my old ways and decided to go for walk. How long had it been since I'd gone for a walk by myself?

"Mr. North?" a woman said from the grand entranceway of the admissions office.

"Yes ma'am," I said, rising from the leather couch.

"My name is Brigit, I will be one the counselors interviewing you today."

"Hi Brigit, thank you so much for this opportunity. What an incredible school, I am blown away," I said, gesturing to the inside of the building.

"Oxford University is a historic institution, Mr. North. We're hoping you'll be a part of it."

"Me too."

* * *

When I returned to the States, my solitary walks would be the thing I missed most. Senior year was a cake walk compared to my previous years of school, leaving plenty of time for reflective strolls and self-discovery—or at least attempted self-discovery. Before I knew it, I was on the other side of Victoria Park with my phone signaling that I needed to be at lunch. *Shit.* I prided myself on my timing, and Leo had commented on how much he liked my punctuality, even though he always arrived just a few minutes earlier than me. I started jogging back through Victoria Park when a bright blue dress distracted me. It was the same little girl I saw last night, wearing the same kind of dress, her mother talking on her phone and carrying the same duffel bag.

Her mother completely ignored her as she sat on a bench tying her shoes. I hesitated—I couldn't just go up to a kid and start talking to her. It didn't look right. I got nervous as I saw them both get up from the bench. Then I received my que—she left her fluffy hair tie on the ground. I sprinted over to grab it and then run after the two.

"Excuse me, excuse me—"

"We aren't interested," the mother snapped without turning.

The little girl glanced behind her and smiled at me. She recognized me from last night.

"Mum, he has my tiara."

"Why does he... oh, thank you. I can't believe she was stupid enough to leave this behind."

"I must tell you what a beautiful dress you have on," I said to the girl. I don't know what came over me—I couldn't stop myself.

"Thank you. My mum made it for me."

"Do you remember me?" I blurted out. I don't know why it was so important that she give me an answer. If I were her age, I would be creeped out by some random guy questioning me like this.

"Do you feel better?" she asked.

"I am feeling much better. Thank you for smiling last night. It was a very nice thing to do."

The mother, talking seriously on the phone, paid no attention to our conversation.

"You looked very sad. My name is Elise. What is yours? Mummy always says that I have to introduce myself when I meet someone new. I couldn't tell you my name last night because you were too far away."

"My name is Landon. Elise is a very pretty name."

"Thank you. Why were you crying last night? I sometimes cry when my teacher is mean to me or when mum yells at me but you're too old to cry for baby things."

"I also cry sometimes. I'm not supposed to cry but sometimes it feels good."

"My mum says that I should not cry but I do it anyways. I feel better after I cry."

Her mother finally turned around and grabbed her hand.

"We must be going. Thank you for bringing that to us," she said, pulling her daughter a few inches forward. She looked to be handling her pretty roughly, but Elise didn't seem to notice.

"If you ever want to cry again, I think you should think of someone who makes you really happy. That's what I do. I think about my dad. He died but he was very nice when he was alive," she said, looking over her shoulder. Then she yanked her hand out of her mother's grip and did the same gesture as last night, a tiny heart.

The new restaurant Leo took me to for lunch wasn't even technically open for business yet, but once again, he knew the owner. I wondered how he'd made such notable friends. In our own cozy corner of the empty place, we kissed for what seemed like an eternity.

"You continue to impress me," I said dreamily, taking a sip of the white wine in front of me. Leo ordered a whole bottle. There were surfboards hung on the walls, checkered cloth on the table, bumper stickers plastered everywhere and the food smelled amazing, like an American diner.

He smiled. "I wanted to bring you today because this is a special occasion."

"How so?"

"I have exciting news."

"What's it about?"

"I know we talked about this summer already and that everything was up in the air, but I just finalized plans—I'm going to Paris."

"That's incredible," I beamed. "Congratulations, Leo. It's all that hard work paying off." I leaned across the table to give him a kiss, and his lips were warm with wine.

"That's not all. Want to know how I got the job?"

"Does it matter? All that matters is that you got it!"

"You helped me get it!"

"No way," I grinned, catching on. "My photos?"

He just smiled. I felt stunned. I never expected those pictures to go anywhere except my personal portfolio. I raised my glass, truly thrilled for Leo and trying to ignore the voice nagging in the back of my head about making a decision for the summer. Time was closing in on me. I wished I could live in this spring for the rest of my life.

"To you," I toasted.

"To us," he corrected.

"To you and your incredible visions that provide you with a life that you truly want. Cheers."

I drank deeply, eager to silence the chaos in my head.

"I want you to come with me," he said then.

The wine went down my trachea instead of my esophagus and I gasped for air, pounding my chest as if that would be any actual help. Leo got up and rushed over to help me, but I held up my hand, *I was fine?* The prolonged coughing fit bought me some time. *Please universe, just give me some more time.*

"You want me to come with you to Paris? Isn't that a really big thing to do?" I managed at last.

"It is." He appeared suddenly small in his chair, bright eyes looking up at me nervously. This was a good man, smart and talented and kind and fascinating and beautiful. And he loved me.

"That is a big decision to consider. Believe me, I am thrilled for you. I can't even tell you how excited I am for you—"

"Then come with me. We can spend a romantic summer in Paris together," he grinned, knowing it was a cheesy line.

"It's just that I have to think about a job for myself. You know I applied for a bunch of jobs in the States, and if I get one that pays enough and has the ability to open doors for me, then I might have to take it," I explained.

"I thought you were going to say that. So I thought ahead." He pulled out his laptop from his bag. I felt my carotid artery pounding in my neck as the screen displayed a page with the words *U.S Embassy and Consulates in France.*

"After you told me about your application for the White House, I talked to a few of my friends and forwarded them your resume."

"How did you get my resume?" I laughed, bewildered.

"I went on the website LinkedIn? You have it up there." He was shy now, embarrassed.

"Oh my gosh, Leo. And what else?"

"My friend said that if you want a job in the Communication Office of the Franco-American Embassy, it's all yours."

A photographer who I met less than a month ago had secured me a job that thousands of students all over the world would kill for. All he wanted in return was to spend the summer with me.

"The only catch is that we're going to have to work on your French, because one of the conditions is that you're able to read and speak some French. My friend says it doesn't have to be a lot, but you have to be able to have simple conversations."

I sat in the shapeless atmosphere of this vast opportunity. There were suddenly no boundaries on the perimeters of my life; no lines I was confined to. There was only one answer that I knew would make me truly, wholly happy.

"I accept," I said.

He froze, like he was prepared to give more of his persuasive speech and now wasn't sure what to do. His fingers hovered over the keyboard. "What?"

"I accept your offer. The only thing I want to talk about is the living situation. I feel it's too early to live together, so I'll find my own place."

I expected more persuasion, but he just nodded. He appeared to be in a daze. I guess I was, too.

"I'm so excited," he whispered, looking at me with tears in his eyes. He had done so much for me, and I had done nothing for him.

"Let's ask for the check and, um, we can eat the food back at your place," I said. I was sure he could feel the blood pounding in my hand that he was holding.

"The chef says he has a whole afternoon prepared. Do you not like it?"

"Leo, I would like to take the food back to your apartment. I want to say thank for what you're doing for me," I said slowly, looking him straight in the eye.

After what seemed like an eternity, he finally understood, but he didn't smile. His cheeks went pink and he looked very serious. It made me feel even more terrified—and also more excited. This was a serious endeavor, after all. The idea that we would treat it with the respect it deserved pleased me.

During the cab ride back to his apartment, I sat beside him sweating. *What am I doing? Do I really want this?* I felt indebted to him—I just wanted to make him happy.

He paid for the cab and I followed him inside. I watched him place the food, still hot, on the kitchen counter. Before he could turn around to face me, I lifted my shirt over my head, desperate to please him. He took my trembling hands in his as if to stop me, or at least slow me down, but it was too late for that. I kissed him hard and dragged him toward the bedroom, repeating to myself that I had to do this, that I would do this right for Leo. How bad could it be?

The next thirty minutes were among the most unpleasant experiences of my life. I hated every second of it, but I loved Leo. He was obviously happy—happy might be an understatement—and I was glad that he fell asleep in my arms afterward. *He cannot see the lie, the façade. I was acting.* As I laid and listened to his steady breathing, I wondered why I couldn't enjoy the experience like he did. I was very much attracted to him, emotionally and physically, but I hated the physicality the entire time. I cared for Leo. I wanted to be with him. But I never wanted to do all that again.

However, now that I'd opened the door, there was no closing it. That would be cruel; he would feel as if he did something wrong. Physical intimacy is crucial to any ongoing relationship, but with no pleasure in anything we did, there was no way for me to see a clear path forward. Maybe the unpleasant losing of one's gay virginity was something all gay men had to endure.

"Well, I'd better get going," I said as we finished the food we'd brought home. I didn't want to seem like I was in too big of a rush, but my fear of a round two occurring drove me toward the door. I placed our plates in the sink and headed toward my shoes.

"Oh, you're leaving?"

My heart throbbed painfully. "I have to get ready for Madrid," I said. It would offer yet another chance to cool off and reconfigure my life.

"Can I see you before you go?"

"I would love to see you before I go."

"How does tomorrow night sound?"

"What about during the day? I'm having dinner with Jake tomorrow," I lied, hoping a daytime event would make sex less likely.

"Works for me."

"I am glad it works for you," I said, kissing him on the lips.

"Landon," he said, studying me as I collected my belongings.

"Leo," I said, trying to feign confidence.

"Thank you."

"No, thank you."

As I walked along the sidewalk, I knew I would no longer be able to say that I was truly straight. It was a lie I had told myself all these years. Despite all the bodily pain I was already experiencing, I felt invincible. This is who I was meant to be. I may not have liked it but breaking that barrier with him gave me more satisfaction than anything else.

Back in my dorm, I called Sidonie to tell her the good news about the summer move. I still had to deal with Jake, but he would understand as long as I told him the White House rejected me.

"I miss you," Sidonie's sweet voice said into my ear. I remembered our nights together in Copenhagen, how easily and naturally our bodies fit together. How she moved against me—it was what we were made for. It was what I was made for.

"I miss you too," I said, and reality sunk back in like a blade. I could not have both.

April in Madrid

The two days in London, before Madrid, passed quickly. I saw Leo, in a public setting this time, so I wouldn't have to entertain the idea of a second hookup. Unbeknownst to me, I kept crossing my arms. He asked me multiple times what was wrong.

"What? Nothing's wrong."

"You only cross your arms when you're pissed, or like, out of it."

He knew me too well. "I just don't want to leave you," I lied, leaning across the park bench to kiss him.

Falling back into the tradition of Donut Time with Jake was a relief I didn't know I needed until I was three donuts deep. Watching Batman: The Dark Knight Rises while scarfing down a box of donuts—two glazed, two Nutella filled and two cruelly named It's Always Gaytime—was the perfect preparation for Madrid. He asked me why I was limping and I told him I'd done squats the day before.

When I told him I didn't get the White House gig, he looked at me gravely.

"Dude, seriously? I can't believe it."

I shrugged. "I know."

In an attempt to make me feel better, he opened a bottle of Johnny Walker Special Edition Gold Label and we made ourselves two of the very classy and extremely versatile whiskey sours, dorm style. We had mastered using everyday objects to make drinks, so when he pulled out the bottle, I emptied a water bottle to be used as a shaker and added the egg, sugar, lemon juice and whiskey. He prepared the glasses with one large ice cube each.

We sipped on those drinks for the rest of the evening. I felt bad for misleading him, but I'd already told Leo he could proceed with securing the job at the French Embassy. Jake was shocked when I told him where I had decided to take my summer internship, saying he didn't even know it was legal for an American intern to work at a French Embassy. He asked me why I had never mentioned it before and I told him it came out of nowhere. He pressed me for further details but I changed the topic.

We talked about Sidonie, and the inquisition continued: How did the last trip go? What did I like about her so much? What did I expect to happen when we returned to the United States? He saw how much fun I had with her at the bar during Saint Patrick's Day but could not understand why I was so passionately involved with her.

I shook my head. "It's different with her," was all I could think to say.

"Man, I wish I could go to Madrid with you guys." His dad was coming to London, which was why he wasn't going to Lana. Madrid was going to be not only a celebration for my twenty-first birthday, but also a work trip. I was signed with two agencies in Spain and had two shoots during the five days I'd be there.

Fortunately, neither of the shoots were on my actual birthday, when I planned to go to the Lana Del Rey concert and get drunk as all hell. All my best friends and roommates from Boston College had decided to study in Spain – Madrid and Barcelona – for the semester, and because work was paying for the trip, I splurged—unbeknownst to Ryan and my other agents—getting a penthouse near the metropolitan center. It was prime location and was large enough to fit Sidonie and myself, as well as all my roommates who wanted to have a break from their homestay families.

Once again, I pushed Leo into a dark corner of my mind for the time being to make room for Sidonie in the spotlight.

She greeted me even more enthusiastically than in Copenhagen, and once again, everyone turned to watch us kiss each other.

"How did you get even more beautiful?" I whispered against her skin on our way to the penthouse. I couldn't wait to peel her dress off and be truly alone.

"I'll never tell," she grinned.

When we opened the door, I was startled to be greeted by all my roommates.

"Landoooo!"

"Yeah, birthday boy!"

The whiskey was passed around, and I introduced everyone to Sidonie. The group; Lane, Nico, Danny, Mark, Izzy, Sophia, Maddie, Will, Sawyer and Catherine all stared at her like she was from another planet. We had become so accustomed to "our group" than any new addition threw off the dynamic—not to mention she was one of the most beautiful people on the planet.

Sidonie effortlessly laughed away their shocked faces; I wanted to take in as much of her as I could.

"Let's go see the master suite," I said quietly, taking her hand.

"Do you like my dress?" she whispered as I closed the door.

I turned to look at her and, in her hand, crumpled into a tiny ball, was the dress she was referring to.

By the time we were done, everyone was dressed and ready to go out. We were decently hammered but scooted our way to the nearest bar while Sidonie talked to everyone. She captivated them with her stories and her charm, entranced them with her accent, amazed them with her beauty and made them fall in love with her every time she spoke. I watched her all night, in my drunken stupor, and fell more and more in love with her. We stayed out all night and when we finally called it quits, we went back to the suite and passed out wherever there was room.

The next morning, I woke up with a wicked hangover and so did Sidonie. We held our heads through breakfast and laughed when we both gagged at the sight of food. There was no way in hell I was going to be hungover for Lana. I had brought my edibles from London and split them amongst everyone before we set out for the day. By noon on April 20th, we were basically a group of the walking dead. I'm still not sure how we made it unscathed through Madrid on electric bikes, but there were no accidents. No one was accustomed to how strong the gummies were, so we sat in a park and listened to a local band for over three hours in the 85-degree heat.

The day passed by and we all became more and more happy. Sidonie continued to intoxicate everyone. As she sped through the park, I realized that my high school relationship had been nothing compared to this.

After the park, she and I went back to the apartment so we could get ready for Lana. It was the last stop on her tour, and the tickets had sold out in a record-breaking thirty seconds, so none of my friends had the chance to secure any. It would just be me and Sidonie, which was exactly what I wanted.

"I don't know if you got my message a few days ago," I said to her as she twirled in front of the mirror. She was wearing a bright yellow dress, perfect for this concert, that clung to her body like a glove. No, not even a glove, it clung to her like spandex. I saw every curve. "About Paris."

"I did get a message," she said, smiling at me through the mirror. I expected her to be more excited—her calm demeanor was off-putting.

"What did you think of it?"

Her smile faltered ever so slightly and my stomach sank. She didn't want me in Paris after all.

"I'm happy about it."

"Are you?"

"Do you think I am?" she said, turning to study me.

"I don't know. I was expecting a different reaction. The opportunity came around and I jumped at the chance but I don't want to intrude. I know Paris is your city and all that, I just thought—"

"Landon. I am very excited you're going to be spending your summer in Paris." She came over to me and straightened out the buttons on my shirt, but there was something in her eyes I couldn't distinguish—something I'd never seen before.

"I just thought—"

"I know what you thought. I know what I think. I'm excited that you're going to spend your summer with me, but…"

"Shit. I knew it."

"No. I was going to call you right back after you left me the message but… what happens when you have to leave? You don't live in France. You don't even live in London. What happens when you leave Europe?" I finally identified what I saw in her eyes—it was fear.

"What do you mean?" I knew what she was referring to, but I wanted to hear her answer to fulfill some selfish part of me.

"It has to end eventually." She wanted me to agree with her to some unspoken covenant that would be solidified right then and there, but again, some selfish, fucked-up part of my brain wanted to enjoy the moments with her so badly that I did the opposite.

"Not necessarily." I regretted the words as soon as they were out of my mouth. I was lying to her now as well.

"What do you mean?"

"Do we have to talk about it right now?" I asked, trying to backtrack.

"I would like to," she said, going back to stand in front of the mirror.

"Then how about you start?"

"If you did spend your summer in Paris, where would you live?"

"Where do you live?"

"No. Don't play that game with me. You and your silly comebacks."

"Then we won't talk about that," I said, smiling at her as she put on her makeup.

"What happens after you leave this summer?" she asked.

"That's a long way away."

"What do you see happening then? If you were to guess right now, what would you guess would happen to us if you left for the States?"

She posed it as if there was a possibility that I would stay in Europe and not return to complete my college education. Things had come so far between the two of us in such a short time. I had met this girl twice but we were talking like we were planning the rest of our lives together. I would very much like to spend my life with her, especially if Leo would agree to be near me. Would I put him on the backburner?

"I would like to be with you as long as I can," I said, which did not answer the question but it did what I wanted it to do. She stopped putting on her makeup and climbed onto me and kissed me. I was hard in a second but she paid no attention. She sat on my lap straddling me and stared.

"I want that too."

Sitting on the edge of the bed, in the yellow room of an Airbnb in Spain, I removed part of my heart and handed it to a girl I had only met three times. I was beginning to feel something, actual emotions, and it made me happier than I could have ever imagined. *I was feeling something.* I wanted to invest myself in this girl and she wanted the same thing. This is what human beings were made for. The emotion rolled over me like a steamroller and the room started spinning, just like it did when I saw the White House acceptance. I was the one changing my life, I was back in charge. She stayed on my lap for just a few minutes but then quickly got up and finished her makeup. She fixed her eyeshadow and then grabbed my hand to drag me to the concert.

Lana was fucking incredible. I had heard that she was not a good live performer but her concert blew me out of the water. Sidonie stayed on my shoulders for the entire time and the experience was unexplainable. As if I needed any more proof of how much Sidonie felt for me, Lana's last song brought the biggest surprise.

"That was fucking amazing!" I said, smiling after she walked off stage after her second encore.

"I am so glad you liked it," Sidonie said looking back up on stage and then to me.

"Thank you so much for coming with me."

"I wouldn't have missed even if you gave away my ticket." She smiled, her green eyes scintillating. How easily she cut right into the core of me.

"Ah, wow." I said, drained of emotion as I pulled out my phone to order the Uber.

"I was hoping we could do something else." She said strongly.

"If you don't want to go out then we could stay in and watch a movie or something."

"I, uh, actually wanted to give you a birthday present." She told me.

"I think you already gave me multiple birthday presents." I winked at her, thinking back to the night before in the master suit.

"Be quiet!" she laughed. "This is more official anyway. Come with me."

As the rest of the crowd was pouring through the double gate entrance of the Palacio Vistalegre, she held my hand and pulled me towards the metal gates on the side of the stage. My heart quickened. Was this where Lana was going to come out before she went to her bus? That would be amazing! Instead of stopping and waiting, she pulled me past the three guards, after flashing them a badge, and we walked behind the curtains. I heard A$AP Rocky's voice before I saw the lights.

"This is my birthday present to you." She ceremoniously pulled the heavy black curtains away from the door. I was standing in the beginning of the after-party. Before me stood A$AP Rocky, Lana del Rey, the entire band and a few others who were presumable important, chatting and laughing casually.

"Sidonie," I began as I turned towards her, starstruck.

"No need to thank me. I didn't do this alone, but I wanted to make sure that this was memorable for you."

"Jesus," I said gawking at the crowd in front of me.

She didn't say anything else but instead strolled right into the party. To my sheer amazement, she went up to Lana and began talking to her. Who was this girl? After an eternity standing in the doorway, I finally swallowed my astonishment and walked after her. Lana was still talking to my girlfriend so I, of course, went up to her and I told her how great her show was. She kissed me on the cheek saying how much she appreciated us coming. She proved it to me – Sidonie was a true Lana del Rey fan. Someone pulled out a joint and we all started smoking it. I was smoking a joint backstage with Lana Del Rey! Then, after too many drinks and another two or three joints, we waved goodbye. The thought of the shoot the next morning sobered me more quickly than I expected. I was going to be bloated from the booze and I already knew that I was going to get shit for it. I also did not want Sidonie to feel obligated to stay with my friends, who would probably sleep until the afternoon, but also did not want her roaming the city by herself.

"Hey, so for tomorrow, what do you want the plan to be?" I said to her as we arrived back at the apartment.

"What do you mean?"

"I have to work so what do you want to do while I am away?"

"I'm coming with you," she said and I snorted. She was joking.

"Funny," I said, "What do you really want to do? I don't know what time I will finish but we could go dancing after I am done. Grab something to eat and then head out for the night?"

"I was not making a joke. You think you are Mr. Hotshot. I am going to come with you tomorrow. I have never been to a photoshoot before and if you are going to be in the spotlight, then I will be part of the entourage. I will stay silent." She looked at me directly, and there was no way to refuse that gaze.

"Then that is settled. We have a 0600 call time. As long as you think you could get up, I would love to have you come with me. I had no idea you were interested."

"It is art, is it not? I like art, do I not?" she said cunningly, raising her eyebrows.

"I will agree with you there," I said, bringing her in close to me. "You are a work of art yourself. They should be taking pictures of you tomorrow."

"By the end of the shoot, they will be," she smiled, skipping in front of me. *Good Lord, how did this happen to me?*

The next day she was up before me; she had showered, dressed, curled her hair, and put on her makeup before I was even done brushing my teeth. Without her I would not have made it on time because even with her help, I walked in to the studio right before the photographer. I had been late to a shoot only once and it was the worst thing imaginable; photographers hate to be left waiting and they will make you feel it.

"Landon, I presume?" The photographer said after he grabbed a preliminary breakfast.

"Pleasure to meet you." I said extending my hand in his direction. He ignored it.

"You know who we are shooting for today, yes?"

"I was made aware." I said. Big name, big day, big payout.

"Then take off your shirt and get there. I don't talk to the models like most photographers. I like to keep a clear distinction between the subject and the process." He said pointing to the center of stage. *Damn, it is way too early for this.*

"This is the other model?" The photographer said, gesturing to Sidonie hanging onto one of the lighting structures. "I thought we had only one today."

"Actually this is..." I smiled as I began to respond to him.

"Yes." She said and my mouth hit the floor.

"Get out there then. What are you waiting for? I don't have all day." He said impatiently.

I panicked. There was nothing I could do. This was a solo shoot for Gabbana. What would the company say if they saw two people in the pictures?

"I am going to get in so much trouble," I whispered to her when she was close enough.

"Relax, I will pretend I got sick and leave in an hour. He will take the photos of you and you will get your money. You Americans and your money, just enjoy the day. The only person that could get in trouble here is me. This is worth the risk." She said, leaving no room for negotiation.

She was a natural, not that it surprised me, but the photographer liked her more than he liked me. He was gay. I stood in the same spot, in practically the same pose the entire time, while the "model I had never met before" draped her body over me in unimaginable ways. An hour in, the photographer was really into it and he did not question anything we were doing. Sidonie had stripped down to a bra and underwear they provided and I was in my underwear as well.

"Are you going to tell him soon?" I said to her when he ordered that we seductively stared into each other's eyes like we were in love.

"No, I am having fun," she said, grinning wildly.

"I know you are, but I could get in a lot of trouble."

"Then say you don't know me. I could be any random person. You showed up here by yourself and I was already here. The photographer made a mistake and none of the assistants have said anything to me yet. This is their fault that they have the wrong models. You did not plan this so you cannot be blamed." She smirked as she moved her body even closer to me. It was when she took that half step towards me, tempting me to say something back to her, that he yelled freeze. This was the picture he wanted. After he was satisfied that he got the perfect shot, he showed us the pictures and they did not disappoint. It was just us, against a white background, in nothing but our brand-name underwear, a palpable tension easily visible on screen. Her eyes glistened and even through my anxiety, I stared at the pictures in admiration. It was back to the commercial feel that I had perfected but this was more elegant because of her. The pictures were nothing like Leo's... Leo. They were nothing like the editorial shoot I did with him, but they were beautiful in their own right.

"Who sent you here again?" an assistant said in French after the photographer had disappeared.

"Mon agent m'a dit d'être ici," she barked.

"Who is your agent?" the Spaniard said, obviously able to understand French.

"What does that concern you?" She glared at him.

"How are you getting paid? It seems that we must have made a mistake. We only asked for one model but here you are. Are you sure you are in the right spot?"

"Wouldn't it be too late to ask me that now? My agent told me to come here and I showed up. I am sorry if I was not supposed to, but I will have a talk with him myself," she said sternly.

Obviously confused, and a little bit afraid, the assistant backed away and apologized.

"This cannot happen tomorrow," I said to her once we were dressed and leaving.

"I am not coming tomorrow. I did it once and I don't need to do it again," she flouted.

"You were trying to get in the shoot all along, weren't you?" I said, finally understanding the purpose of the accompaniment.

"I wanted to try it once. Don't tell me that you did not like it. I saw what was happening in your underwear, Mr. Calvin Klein." She pulled me out of the studio and into a cab. "Now, let's go get food because I want to go dancing."

The rest of the Madrid weekend felt as if I was floating down a lazy river. Not a single thing went wrong, time moved at exactly the right pace, and I worried about nothing except her. I felt more protective of her now than I did before. It wasn't until the last few seconds with her that I began to panic. When was I going to see her again?

"I will come on your next trip if you want me," she said.

"I don't even know where I am going yet."

"Isn't that the fun in it?"

"For some people it is."

"Then I guess I am some people." We stood in between the two airport terminals. She was taking a later flight back to Paris and wanted to spend more time outside before she was crammed on a plane.

"I will miss you."

"Tu vas me manquer mon amour," she responded with a light kiss on my cheek, "until I see you again."

"Until I see you again," I echoed as I entered the airport. This is what I wanted for the rest of my life. I wanted her.

The summation of April

"Mom," I said hesitantly into the phone. It had been almost three months since I talked to her.

"Landon, I thought you were not going to call your mother. You know, the woman who gave birth to you and spent twenty years trying to make you into a person that the world will be proud of?"

"Here I am, but I wanted to make this short so I don't waste your time. I'm extending you a courtesy to let you know that I have accepted a summer internship in Paris. I will not be coming home."

"You accepted the job already?" she asked after a short pause.

"Yes." I said curtly.

"Without speaking to me first? This is by no means a courtesy call then; this is a call to shove this in my face. After all that I have done for you, and you don't even run this by me? How are you going to support yourself over there? What are you going to be doing? Your siblings are going to be devastated that you are not coming home. Does your father know about this?" She scoffed cynically. "No, how stupid of me to ask. Of course he knows about this. You tell him everything and you tell me nothing. This is one of your stupidest decisions yet."

"Dad does not know about it and by definition of a courtesy call, that is exactly what I am doing. In regards to everything else, I have it all figured out," I lied, waves of stress and adrenaline pumping through me as they always did when I spoke with her.

"Landon, you are *not* going to stay over there."

"It is too late for your input. I am staying over here."

"And what? You are going to model to support yourself? No one in the business world is ever going to take you seriously if you continue to do that. How many times do I have to tell you all of this?"

"I got an internship in the American Embassy in Paris. I am staying here."

"You are lying. What are you actually doing?" Her cold voice cracked through the phone. She considered my modeling a passing stint, an adolescent infatuation, that I would eventually become embarrassed of once I grew up. The prestige of her own job relegated everyone else around her to a lesser role. She was addicted to the pomp of her position.

"I am working in the communication office in the American Embassy in Paris."

"We will see about that."

"How, Mom? How will we see about that? I have secured the internship, it is paid, and housing is cheap. How can this possibly be not good enough?"

"You know how. I know when you are lying Landon. You just want a free pass in life. You just want to go to the gym then take off your clothes for all these gay photographers and then have pictures so you can post on Instagram or Facebook…uh, whatever you kids do these days. You know the only reason those guys get into taking pictures is so they can take advantage of you later on. You may not be telling me the truth, but you should know by now that I find everything out."

"I will email you the acceptance letter. It is not like I am asking you to come over here and help me move in or anything. I am simply keeping you informed of what is going on."

"This is a bad move. One day, you are going to wake up and see how much pain you have caused your family. I don't know when that day is going to be, but when it comes I will not be here to comfort you."

"How do you possibly think that staying over here is causing any of you pain? Colman is going to be in Los Angeles, Molly is going to Virginia Tech for pre-season training in June, and Kendall will be splitting her time between you and dad. How does that hurt anyone?" I said exasperatedly, my pulse beating.

"You are going to kill your grandparents. They are going to die while you are away."

"Good Lord, do you ever give it a break?" I shouted, unable to contain myself any longer. "Good luck trying to find a way to prove that I don't have the internship." I slammed the phone down. This was the exact reason I did not speak to her. Landing an internship in any embassy, regardless the national affiliation, would be good enough for any other family on Earth. Not for mine. I almost didn't want to call my dad but I knew that if I left him out of the picture, he'd feel betrayed.

"Dad," I said, trying to regain my chipper tone.

"Buddy! Great to hear your voice. How is everything? I saw on Instagram or Snapchat that you went to see Lana for your birthday! How awesome was that? Tell me all about it."

Even though I talked to him four or five times a week, he always acted as if he hadn't spoken to me in decades. It seemed that today he was in a good enough mood, so I told him everything about Lana, leaving out the part about Sidonie because it was not my parents' privilege to know what was happening in my love life.

"How amazing is that? Was she just as hot in person?" he asked eagerly.

"You don't even know."

"Oh good…but did you call just to check up or is something else going on? How is all your budgeting going on over there? I can move more money if you need me to."

"No, no, the money is great, Dad. Thank you for the offer though. No, I just wanted to call to let you know that I am not coming home this summer. I got an internship over here."

"What?" he gasped, the disappointment in his voice palpable. After the affair and then the divorce, my mom guilted my siblings into staying with her and told them horrible lies about my dad. Now, my siblings wanted nothing to do with him and he was alone in our house. He was counting on me coming home this summer to keep him company.

"I got an internship at the American Embassy in Paris. I think it would be a great opportunity for me," I repeated hesitantly, trying to feel good for myself while imagining how lonely he'd be.

"Yes…" he said slowly, galvanizing himself for my sake., "Yes, I think that is really great, buddy. I am really proud of you. This is all your hard work paying off. Do you need help finding a house or money for food? I know you have your modeling money, but let me know if there is anything I can help with. I would be more than happy to come back over to move in if you want. I know I am going to see you in a few weeks anyway for Morocco, but just keep me updated."

"Will do, Dad," I said softly, my heart expanding and retracting with mixed emotions.

"One more thing… does your mother know?" He was still in love with her even after all the crap she had put him through. It annoyed the shit out of me and each time he asked about her, it made me angry. He should hate her for what she did, yet, he still loved her at the end of the day. I couldn't understand how any kind of love could withstand such brutality.

"Yes. I told her and she said it was fine. I already accepted the position and there is nothing that she could have done about it. She doesn't believe me, but I guess she will have to deal with that on her own."

"Good. Good, I think that was a good call. Have you been speaking to her a lot or..."

"Bye, Dad."

"Okay, I get it. Thank you for telling me! Talk to you soon, buddy. I am glad Madrid was so much fun."

I hung up and threw myself onto my bed, both conversations exactly what I expected.

"Oh Lord," I sighed to myself as my phone rang. *Which parent needed more from me?*

"Landon!"

"Leo."

"I know you just got back but I have a last-minute favor."

"What can I do for you?"

"I need you tomorrow morning at 10 AM at Big Sky."

"For what?" This would be the third day of shooting. He had my attention because Big Sky is the largest studio in all of London, but I wanted to scarf down some burgers and chicken livers right about now.

"The model for the shoot got sick last night and just bailed on me. I am a guy short and this is a big production."

"I will absolutely help you out, babe. I will see you then."

"You are wonderful. I cannot wait to see you and hear all about Madrid. I hope it was a wonderful time."

"It truly was. I cannot wait to see you." I said and I meant it, feeling the excitement tingling in my chest already.

The next morning, I rolled out of bed at 0600 to prep for Big Sky. Luckily, I hadn't gorged myself during my time in Madrid, so I wasn't bloated – I looked in as good of shape as ever. I had missed Leo. There were so many things that reminded me of him when I was in Madrid. When I was out to lunch, there was a table of Italians all drinking Limoncello after their dinner, a drink he made me fond of. Then when I was in the park I saw a man walking around taking pictures of birds, the photographer squinting his eyes exactly as Leo did when he was focusing on the subject. I was nervous for the shoot, as each time I shot with the same photographer, I could see the evolution of our relationship in the pictures. It intrigued me and alarmed at the same time. How would Leo see me now knowing this was for a client, not for personal pleasure?

"Hi, babe," I said once he rushed over to me after I entered the studio.

"We cannot do that today," he said quickly, looking around.

"Okay, it was not like I was going to publicly call you that today." I smirked but also feeling slightly hurt by the intensity in which he told me.

"No, we can't do any of that today. I have a lot of people watching me and they can't know that I asked my boyfriend to be the subject. It will give them the impression that I only know how to work with people I know."

"Calm down, you are going to do great. Believe me when I say that I was not going to say anything about our relationship. I will be on my best behavior."

"Okay, thank you…just, please try," he flustered.

"Excuse me?" I quipped shortly, "You think I do not try any other time? Who is this for, anyway?" I looked at the throng of people gathered behind him. The studio was huge with a plain charcoal grey tarp as the background. This was going to be extremely editorial and was, by far, one of the largest productions I had ever been a part of but his demeanor was pissing me off.

"Vogue." He shuttered, then quickly turned as I absorbed the weight of the name.

"I need all the models on set please," a bald-headed man yelled from the background. It was not even 0930 and they were already calling us to set? Even worse, there were three other male models that looked like they could be my brothers.

Who would the photographer like the best?

"First we want to get a few single shots before we put you all together," the bald-headed man yelled. He had an American accent but he was definitely not from the States. He carried himself as if he belonged sitting in a throne in Versailles eating grapes out of a servant's hand. The three other models went first, and watching Leo work with them heaped more pressure onto me. It wasn't until the second model stripped down into his Moschino underwear that I saw that Leo was actively flirting with them as he worked. I couldn't even tell that they were gay when I introduced myself. My gaydar is normally excellent, and when I noticed his actions, I turned red. Did he do this with every one of his subjects? I get that photographers have to make the models feel comfortable, but this was uncalled for, especially in front of me. The crew of assistants and directors standing behind Leo seemed pleased with the shots, which made it even worse. The other guys moved in front of the camera, and not only were they more shredded than me, but they looked effortless posing for him. I knew that was not how I would look.

"I have seen enough. Thank you, Jamie," the bald-headed man snorted to the last model. Jamie smiled and walked off to change into the Versace clothes, his easy self-assuredness making me feel even more nervous.

"We have one more, yes?" the man asked Leo.

"I believe so. I don't know where he is," he said, pretending to look around for me.

"There he is," an assistant pointed.

"Good, then bring him here. Oh, his abs need a little work – make sure to put some oil on them please," the director critiqued.

They had already found something wrong with me – unbelievable. I looked at Leo to see if he would say something, but he just looked listlessly at me, as if he would agree if it made him look better in front of these important people. After the baby oil was applied, I walked past Leo and into the center, hoping to get this over with as soon as possible. It had been years since I felt so out-of-place on set.

"Hi, I'm Leo. It is very nice to meet you." He caught me by the arm as I strode past him. If he wanted to play it like this, then I would too.

"What's up, my man? I'm Landon, nice to meet you." I retorted casually, shaking his hand with iron strength so much that I saw his lips flatten as he felt the pain of my grip.

"We don't have all day. Leonardo, is this how you always work?" the bald man squawked.

"I just want to make sure that the model feels comfortable."

"My name is Landon, not *the model*," I sneered.

"Yes, sorry," Leo said genuinely. The wretched guilt in his eyes was enough for me. Perhaps his distance felt even worse than normal because he was the one to come onto me first, and now that I accepted it was that much easier for him to reject me. It was a strange feeling, and not a good one to have when you're supposed to be one of the most confident and sexy people on the planet.

"I have been ready. Let's go. I'm sorry, what did you say your name was again?" I snapped, the desire to see him hurt mounting inside of me.

"Whatever you want to call me is fine," he said, backing off the mat while looking at his camera. I could see a flicker of strangeness move vaguely through his expression. Was I winning yet?

"What direction do you want me to go with this?" I asked, addressing the bald guy instead of Leo.

"Great question, Landon," the director said.

Leo didn't say anything, breathing heavily through his nose as his hands shook over his camera. He was scared that I was going to sabotage him, pissed that I wasn't helping him in the way I promised. But the sting of his words and flirtations couldn't leave me just yet. I felt things for this young Italian that I did not feel about anybody else. He deserved way more than I was giving him, but he couldn't treat me like a stranger when he wanted and a lover when no one was looking. *Even though that is exactly what I was doing to him.*

"Leo?" The director repeated.

"Um, yes, well…" he stuttered, still fiddling with the settings on his camera.

"I will start like the other guys so he can get a feel for me," I said, coming to his defense, suddenly blushing for him.

"Thank you, I mean, yes, I think that would be good."

I stayed in front of the camera for another twenty minutes before the director pulled me aside and told me that the pictures exceeded his expectations. By the time I was done with the first set, the entire production crowded around watching Leo. The other guys were furious.

"We are going to make you the center of the shot. You'll have to go change into the clothes, but you are perfect. We'll need to remove some of your stomach fat in post-production, but you have the look we are going for. The photographer…"

"*Leo,*" I corrected.

"Yes, well, Leo seems to have a special connection with you. It is like you two share a special bond. That is very rare to see in pictures, but I know how to pick the winner. Go, quickly change into the clothes and come right back out. We have a busy day."

He was right. The eight hours on set were exhausting. Leo was required to constantly change the props and background as he saw fit – by himself. *They are really testing him.* Slowly I began to feel more comfortable in tandem with Leo. Because they clearly approved of his artistic direction, I began to feel more confident. Eventually I became more at ease than I would have ever been before. With his direction, we used our bodies to make true artwork. The environment, the people, and the product were perfect; it was all in sync.

"Okay guys, now I want you to imagine something. Pretend like you are children. Imagine that you are helpless in the arms of one another, but make it seem like there is also a god towering over you. I don't want to see any fear but try to exhibit some type of controlled spontaneity as you defy this god." Leo said, his dark eyes penetrating as he looked toward us, tilting his head to find the light. It was insanely attractive to see him at work in the flow of his artistic process.

"Who is the god?" I asked, trying not to smile.

"No one is. Imagine that it is greater than the four of you. I want to see some defiance but the realization that you are utterly helpless in the arms of another. This is the theme we are going for, for this company and the magazine, but I haven't seen it yet. On my count, I want you to keep moving, but pretend you are children. Go!" he yelled, then the four of us threw our bodies over each other– not in an artificial way, but in a way that conveyed the idea that we were lounging around with our best friends. It did not work.

"Okay, that wasn't what I was going for but it looked better," he sighed, nodding rapidly and furrowing his brows. "How about imagining that you are children, but not normal children; you are angels and you just fell from power. You are mightier than humans but are completely drained of all the godly powers. Yes, let's try that." He moved into position again, fumbling with the camera and wincing. We tried the next position but that, again, did not work.

"Okay, how about–" he began, but the director cut him off.

"Enough. This is not working. This is not what I wanted to see. Everyone take a break. Leo, can I see you please?" His pale face grimaced as Leo followed him to the side.

"Blimey, what more does he want us to do? We've been at this for hours now! I can't believe we have not gotten the bloody shot yet!" Jamie groaned, titling his head back into exasperated hands.

I watched Leo's shoulder slump as he apologized to the irate director who was gesticulating madly like he was trying to flick grease off his fingers. I wanted to come to Leo's defense seeing him the way he was on the first day we met– barefoot with a camera hanging around his neck, shirt pressed against his lean body. All of those once-mysterious qualities had so quickly become endearing to me.

"Look," I said to the group of guys behind me, "I know what he wants. I need you to listen to me. Imagine that there are three different forms of the body: a god, the hero, and the child..." I explained, trying to enlighten them as quickly as possible.

"Everybody back on set!" The director yelled minutes later, storming away from Leo. Leo returned with his head down, cracking his knuckles anxiously.

"Let's try this again," Leo started nervously, clearing his throat. "Imagine..."

"We got it," I interjected, nodding.

"I want you to imagine that you are made of water..."

"I think we got it," I repeated as Leo looked awkwardly at us, peering at the director from the corner of his eye.

"Fine," he sighed, lifting his lips into a soft, closed smile that held within it the weight of his entire career. "On my count: three, two, one, go!"

We fell into perfect position.

The pictures were even more elegant than the ones he took before. They were not as editorial-esque or as feminine, but they captured the clothes in a different way which I knew would make waves. Everyone was visibly exhausted by the time we were let out, and I thanked the director for the day and started to leave.

"What did you say to them?" Leo asked curiously, catching

up with my pace out the door. The director had just exclaimed how brilliant he was as an artist and announced to the room that he would be a photographer to keep their eyes on. I was proud of him.

"What do you mean?" I feigned, trying to look innocent and unaware.

"I saw you talking to them when I was being yelled at. What did you say to them?"

"Well," I smiled, "someone brilliantly told me that there are three main poses for men: the god, the child, and the hero."

"You didn't," he beamed, his face alighting. He looked more joyful than I'd ever seen him, his cheeks reddening.

"That is what made it work and was entirely your fault," I winked at him then grabbed my bag.

"Landon!" he called after me.

"And you even remembered my name this time," I smiled.

"I am sorry. It was a mistake," he flushed.

"You did a great job today and deserve everything that happened. I will meet you at your apartment."

May

French lessons began the day after the Vogue shoot. Leo worked tirelessly – crafting lesson plans, making flashcards, buying French movies, etc. – to make sure I was prepared for the internship. Not only was my neck on the line but his was as well. There was no interview for the position; the embassy simply gave it to me after I passed the background check. Our lessons started out with the basics which, I was surprised to find, I had previously mastered. My accent, which I normally used to mock French people, was well-tuned, and although he said that I acted too American, I would be able to pass in the embassy. The way he spoke did not have the same effect on me as Sidonie. Hers was effortless and silky whereas Leo's was tight and had hints of Italian. They were both fluent and the accent mirrored who they were as human beings. But each time Leo spoke, I found myself thinking of Sidonie.

"Leo," I said after the fifteenth day of consecutive practice.

"Oui?" he answered, raising his eyebrows playfully.

"My dad is coming over in two days and we are going to Morocco. I won't have service. I think I mentioned this."

"Excusez-moi?" he said without looking up from his computer screen.

"Uh!" I sighed before obliging. "Mon père arrive dans deux jours afin que nous puissions aller au Marocco. Je n'aurai pas de service."

"Good, but you shouldn't worry because Morocco is a French-speaking country so you can practice there. Plus, the country is called Maroc. I can always call you at night." He rubbed his hand along my back, and I sighed, looking away from him. I wasn't ready for my two worlds to collide, to explain myself to anyone, for any labels to be suddenly cast upon me. The love and affection that existed between us was too precious to be revealed and subsequently ripped apart by the outside world– let alone my own family.

"I don't think that is a good idea," I said nervously, looking up to him sheepishly.

"Why not?"

"I just don't think it would be a good idea to call you *every* night," I said, trying to hedge the larger issue at hand. "Plus I don't even know when I'll have service. We're staying in the middle of nowhere."

"Okay, then what about every other day? I know we've spent the last fifteen days together, but I thought it was going well. You're getting sick of me already?" He turned to face me, his frank eyes impossible to confront. He pried with his gaze since the first time I met him. There was no escaping him if he wanted to see you.

"I've been loving our time together," I tried, rubbing my hands together nervously. "I just don't think it would be a good idea for you to call me. Then my dad will ask who I was speaking with and then I would have to make something up." I studied his face to see if he understood without my having to explicitly say it, but he just furrowed his brows and shook his head gently.

"Why do you have to make something up? Just tell him who you are speaking to and he will understand," he pleaded gently.

"Leo, I just don't think that will work."

"Why not?"

"I still have not told them about us and…" I sighed, trailing off and shrugging helplessly.

"Oh my God." He rubbed his temples, his head low in his hands. "You told me that you were going to tell him!"

"I just don't know how to!"

"You open your fat American mouth and say that you have a boyfriend!" he shouted back angrily. "It is actually not that hard…questo è incredibile, dopo tutto quello che ho già fatto!"

"Wow," I said, "that was uncalled for."

"Why do you not want to tell your parents that we are together?" He pressed his fingers into his head, staring at me with love and hurt.

"They wouldn't understand," I said solemnly. "They aren't those types of people."

"You told me you had a great relationship with your dad. Why can't you tell him?"

I shook my head, unable to speak. This was the conversation I'd been dreading since he sparked that strange feeling within me. Here was the naked shame I'd been trying to dodge since I first kissed him. I thought if I kept the truth of my sexuality safely outside of language, I'd never have to confront it directly in the outside world. It was so easy to be in love with him that I never sat down to think about the implications of the culture. When you recognize the beauty in somebody the last thing you expect is to be condemned or judged for it– though, of course, I knew it would come eventually.

"It's still so taboo in the states to be… it's not like over here where you can be whoever you want!" I said, frustrated, dissatisfied with my explanation as it came out of my mouth.

"No. You can be whoever you want anywhere, at any time. A place doesn't trigger that change– you do." He averted his gaze, his knuckles tensing. His strong, angular jaw clenched in frustration. He was beautiful at every moment, which only made this moment more painful.

"You just don't know my parents. They'll get upset and then take it out on my siblings, and I can't have that. Then my grandparents would find out and that would kill them." I thought back to the conversation with my mother.

"Babe," he said seriously.

"Don't call me that right now."

"*Honey*," he repeated, catching my eye.

"Leo, this is serious."

"I am going to tell you something," he stopped, pinning my gaze with his. "Life is short, but people spend so much of that time depriving themselves of things they really want. Why should we deprive ourselves of the things we want, when it is those things that we really want that make us special? You need to make sure you let yourself be special because that is why people love you. They are only going to love you for who you *truly* are."

The pause that followed was almost unbearable. He knew he was right. I knew he was right. I was too scared to tell my parents because that would widen the already massive gap in our relationship. My relationship with my parents had changed after everything they had put us through, but I still counted on them, and I didn't know if we could survive another reason for estrangement.

"I will think about it," I said softly after seeing that he had gone back to editing.

"Landon," he said twenty minutes later, after I had finally re-concentrated on the French text in front of me.

"Leo."

"There is something else I wanted to ask you."

"I promise that I will actually think about it. I am not just saying that," I said eagerly, anticipating his next move.

"I know you will. It is something else." He closed his laptop and took off his glasses.

"Yes?"

"I wanted to ask you something…" He dropped his head and rubbed his thumbs over his hands.

"Is everything okay?"

His whole-body language had changed. I had never seen him look so small. Normally he was confident and quirky, but now he was defenseless. His hands were folded neatly in his lap, his shoulders were hunched forward. I could not catch his eye, and his chest was collapsing in and out like a jellyfish.

Two minutes of silence passed, with me staring at him and he staring at the floor. "Are you actually going to Morocco?"

That was the last thing I expected him to ask me. I was baffled. *Where the hell else would I be going?* I continued to stare at him, but he would not look at me.

"Yes. I am *actually* going to Morocco. What an absurd question to ask," I said, but there was something else he was waiting to ask me.

"I just wanted to ask. I know that we have only known each other for a few months and you are a student and not from here… Actually, forget it. I just overthink things." He quickly flipped open his laptop, clearing his throat and scrolling.

"Ask me what you really want to ask me," I said strongly. *Does he still feel the need to conceal things? Shit, I am such a hypocrite.*

"Are you cheating on me?" he finally asked.

The wind knocked out of me as soon as he asked it. My hands began to tremble, my face blanched with a terrible heat. Suddenly all those shrouded, secret parts within me felt flayed open and naked for everyone to see. Thank God he was not looking at me. He would have been able to tell everything immediately if he was looking at me in that moment. He would have seen directly who was sitting behind this precarious façade I'd been trying to delicately construct for myself. He would have known.

"You think I am cheating on you?" I said shakily.

"Yes. I am sorry to ask you, but I just want to know. I don't love you any less, but I thought it was a fair question," he said sheepishly. I'd never seen him so muted and vulnerable before. It made me feel acidic to be the source of his meagerness. That I had the power to turn a lively spirit into this deflated form horrified me. I was the reckless Don Juan, the impetuous hero, and he the curdled child.

"Why...why do you think that?" I stuttered.

This time he looked at me. His gaze sent a cold shock up my spine, flensing from me every hiding spot. I was bare before him, with nowhere to go, nothing to say. In his gaze I was confronted with myself.

"I know I am paranoid but... I love you, Landon. I know that you don't love me and that is fine but–"

"Leo," I tried to interrupt him but he held up his hand.

"Please, don't lie to me. I know that you don't love me as much as I love you. That is okay– I actually think that is how relationships are supposed to work. I am so happy every time that we are together, but I see it in the way you look at me sometimes that you are thinking about someone else. That is okay, really, it is. I know that being with another guy is new to you and that is also okay. You have given me so much time and effort. I just wanted to ask because sometimes when we are together, we are actually not together and I can see it in your eyes. You also travel a lot, and I know that it is for work, but there are a lot of even handsomer guys out there and even though you are telling me that you chose me–"

"Stop." I held up one hand, catching my breath. I was reeling with this flood of thought, unaware that he had been bottling up so much. It was overwhelming.

"No. I have been thinking about it for a while. I don't want to break up, but I want to know. When you travel, I don't talk to you and I think that is how you want it. I know how special you are and so many other people see that, but I want to know for myself so I am not in the dark for longer than I have to be."

He paused but I waited for him to finish. I just looked at him. I nodded at him, waiting for him to add whatever else he had, my heart bleating inside my chest.

"I also noticed that when you came back from Copenhagen and Madrid that you had makeup on your neck," he said, immediately adverting his eyes and sighing. I could tell that he was finally done speaking.

"I promise that there are no other guys Leo... honestly." I reached toward him. Even though it was an honest statement, I had said something which could never be taken back. I was deceiving him. I was deceiving him and it was easy; I was in a position to tell the truth and lie at the same time. Lying was easier than revealing to myself and to him in the same moment that I was not as good as either of us thought. Lying was easier than being confronted with the hurt that would open in him if I were to tell the truth. Better to throw the skeleton back into the closet than to feel truly ugly for the first time in my life.

"I just noticed the makeup on your neck and I thought that you were covering up hickeys," he admitted awkwardly, but I could tell that he was already starting to feel better. He pulled at his lips thoughtfully.

"I promise that I would not lie to you about this. I have enjoyed you so much that I cannot even tell you how much." I sat next to him on the couch, grasping his shoulders and watching his handsome profile.

"You have?" His voice was soft and dark like a bruise.

"More than you could ever know." I kissed him on the lips. It was a small, quick kiss, but it was powerful. It was a reassurance that I was telling the truth. I had even convinced myself that I was telling the complete truth because the kiss was completely innocent. And I really did care deeply for him; that I could not lie about.

"What was the makeup for then?" he asked after pulling back.

"I get bit by bugs a lot and when I am working. The neck is one of the places all you photographers focus on, so I have to make sure there are no dots." I did not tear my eyes from his, hoping my forwardness would convince him.

"You get bit by bugs?" he repeated cautiously, but I had already lied. I could see my reflection in his eyes, an unavoidable mirror.

"Yes," I said confidently.

"And when you travel, you are actually visiting friends?"

"Yes. Haven't I shown you the pictures?"

"Yes, you have," he nodded gently. I could see that my reassurance was making him feel much better. I rubbed my thumbs against his shoulders, trying to conjure him back to me.

"Would you like to see them again?" I smiled at him.

"No. I believe you. I was just so worried that I was not doing a good job."

"Stop! I let you talk before, but now I'm putting my foot down. I cannot adequately tell you how much you mean to me. You have taught me so much and have helped me fall in love with myself. You need to believe me because you are the only guy in my life and I want it to stay that way."

He reverted back to the Leo I knew. When he looked at me, I saw the familiar glint in his eyes which replaced the sadness that had been there just moments before.

"Then don't tell me in words." He leaned in for another kiss, pushing his hands through my hair. I went along with it, and I made him believe it, but the rest of the time together that day, and all the days going forward, I knew that I was going to have to tell him eventually. I loved him that much. But I also knew it would be that much worse to tell him now that I had passed up an open opportunity to come clean. It would feel like that much more of a betrayal.

* * *

The trip to Maroc was much needed. Much to my amazement, my dad genuinely surprised me. I had been talking about traveling in a caravan across the Sahara Desert since I had first seen it on Planet Earth when I was eight years old. For the final leg of our trip, we spent five days in the Sahara traveling by camel to campsites throughout the desert – it was breathtaking and emotional. Each night, after everyone went to bed, I went out onto the dunes and sat in the sand tornados beneath the moon while I played Odesza. It bordered on a religious experience because there was nothing around me. I couldn't hear myself speak because the wind was so loud, the giant dunes around me threatened to bury me, and the moon floated completely out of reach of everything. The whole experience made me feel small, but most importantly it made me feel human. I understood why the early travelers put so much faith in the sky; the sky was the only place of refuge and peace in the entire world in an environment like the desert. Some nights, I could make out my reflection in the stars. It was what I needed, and I told both Sidonie and Leo the exact thing when they asked me.

Upon my return to London, I was shocked for the second time to find that Leo had planned a trip for us to his hometown in Italy. Initially, I was against the idea because I was exhausted from the desert, but I knew that I could not refuse. While I am not able to remember what I was feeling at the time, I knew this was a turning point in our relationship. It was one of those obstacles that would no longer loom over us. Meeting someone's family was a huge step, but I wasn't nervous.

We landed at San Francesco d'Assisi Airport and took a train to Orvieto in Umbria. The flight was reasonable and the train ride was even shorter. As we chugged by the quaint Italian villages scattered amongst the sweeping fields of mustard-colored flowers, we did not say anything to each other. I opted to study him instead of filling the time with pointless conversation. He told me that he had only been back a handful of times since he started traveling, and when he did come back, it was only because someone close to him had died. As the train sped along the single-rail track towards our destination, the landscape mirrored Leo's emotions.

His demeanor changed the minute we pulled into the station. He was more quiet than usual, but he flashed a smile in my direction every once in a while in order to calm me. When he finally told me that the next stop was Orvieto, his hometown, I could see the tension strung throughout his body. His arms were laced with straight lines of sinew and muscle from clenching and unclenching his fists. His shoulders were so close to his ears that his collar bone was protruding in a way that made it seem like he was anorexic. In the distance emanated a slab of rock that was noticeably out-of-place with the rest of the landscape.

Whereas the Italian countryside was soft and lush, this piece of rock was barren on all sides and looked impossible to scale. I felt the momentum of the train slow and I followed his lead when he got up to collect his bag. I told him that I was excited to meet his family, but he only gave me a curt nod and an *uh-um* in response. We got off the train and the slab of rock looked even more daunting that it had seemed from the train. There was only one way up and one way down. Both were catered by an elevator car that putted slowly up the side. From where we stood, a tower was visible as it jutted into the blue sky. The town looked massive and small at the same time.

"Okay," he finally said before we got out of the elevator car.

"Okay," I said, smiling back at him. He was nervous to be home; I could relate to that.

"Okay. Okay." He looked at the top of the tower, wringing his hands.

"Okay. Okay. Okay."

"Okay. Okay…" he repeated, unaware of what he was doing.

"Leo," I said, cutting him off before he could repeat himself indefinitely.

"Sì scusa."

"That will probably be the extent of my Italian," I said, reminding him to speak in English.

"My fault…" he said thoughtlessly, still fixating on the tower. "I am going to take you to my home. This is where I grew up. I don't know who is home. I did tell them that I was coming."

"Then I am sure they are expecting you. There is nothing to worry about," I tried to reassure him.

"My family does not speak very good English. I will translate for you. My mom speaks French so you can practice with her. She, uh, has never met any one of my partners," he said when the elevator finally stopped and we were told to disembark.

The final comment hit me like a grenade. Why was I the only one he had ever brought to his home? Why was I the chosen one to meet his family? I had only known him for a couple of months and now I was taking a step that, in his twenty eight years, he had never done before? I felt sick to my stomach because not only had I lied to him, but I excelled at it so much he felt it was time for the most important people in his life to meet me. I clenched the railing in the cable car as it jolted upwards and I looked to see where it was going – straight up the side of a cliff. It was the epitome of the town built upon a hill. This was truly a shining beacon on top of pure rock– a fitting place for someone as beautiful and mysterious as Leo.

When we had finally reached the top and as we walked through the worn-down cobbled streets, twisting and turning through the narrow passageways with our bags, Leo stopped each time he saw someone he knew. He did not introduce me to each one of them, which was more than fine by me. I couldn't imagine that there were many people living here, especially seeing as it did not look like a young city.

We passed a grand cathedral at the very top where I could see for miles in any direction. Leo told me that it was a Roman Catholic church dedicated to the Assumption of the Virgin Mary. Each Sunday, tourists and residents of the town would dress in their finest clothes and attend mass together. Then afterwards, they would all go for lunch in one of ten cafes in the city. It was a tradition that dated back to the inception of the city and it was one of Leo's fonder memories growing up. When we passed, I was forced to crane my neck and bend backwards so I could see the entirety of the building. I could not believe that such a monstrosity was created on a bed of solid stone and had existed for so many years.

We stood together, in the empty square, hand in hand for a few minutes. I waited a few seconds so I could take in the moment by myself. It was a town built on rock and guarded by God. The concluding leg of the journey included another ten-minute walk past a vineyard and three cafes when finally, he stopped in front of a quaint house. The house was covered in green vines; they snaked from the foundation to the windowsills and disappeared into the crevices of the stone. There was a birdcage with three songbirds in the bottom window by the kitchen, and another window welcoming strangers into an ornately furnished living room. He knocked on the door three times and when no one answered, he pushed his way in. He needed no key; his front door was simply unlocked.

"Sono a casa. Mama sei que?" he said.

I was about to let out a sigh of relief when no immediate answer came but was halted when I heard footsteps creak down wooden steps.

"I have not seen her in a long time. I will speak to her first but I know that she is going to want to speak to you. Don't let her intimidate you," he said, but when I looked at him, he was in a trance– almost as if he was rehearsing what he was going to say.

"Leonardo, figlio mio! Bentorato a casa mia piccolo!" an elderly woman's voice squeaked from around the corner. From the creaking of the wooden boards, I could tell that she was hurrying down the steps. I immediately started clawing at the cuticles in my fingers. What was I going to say to her? Then I saw her and all my anxiety washed away. She was dressed in a brightly colored shawl, open-toed sandals, and a dress. Her skin was the color and texture of the olive branches that I had seen on my way up the cliff, and on her face was a smile whittled by God himself. I don't know what I expected, but her teeth glowed in her mouth and her eyes twinkled like the stars. As she trotted forward, her smile got even larger and her arms were outspread like angel wings. There was moisture in her eyes, and as she approached him, that moisture turned into tears, dripping happily down her face.

"Mamma," Leo said smiling, intercepting the older woman as she wrapped her arms around him. There was so much love in that room that I panicked and looked for the exits. I wanted to run back out the door and down the side of the cliff; I was interrupting something so pure that my presence here could only be perceived as negative. They hugged for five minutes without letting go of one another. She cried into his shoulders and he stood there stroking her back with his eyes closed. When they had finally broken apart, his mother's eyes still plastered on him, he shook his head and cleared his throat, remembering that I was in the room.

"Mamma, voglio presentarti il mio fidanzato Landon." He gestured to me.

His mother immediately snapped herself out of whatever trance Leonardo had put her in, and I felt the blood drain from my face. This was the moment of truth. In such an old traditional town, surely his mother would look at me and smile and feign niceties while simultaneously cursing him for bringing me here. Or maybe she would ignore me because her son had brought home another guy instead of a girl. Maybe she was going to turn her back to me. As I dug deeper into the beds of my fingernails, waiting for one of these reactions, I exhaled when she rushed towards me and wrapped her arms around me as she did for her own son. I did not say anything and neither did Leo.

She hugged me tighter and tighter, whispering something in Italian to me as the minute passed by. She pulled me down to her height and kissed me on each cheek, both hands wrapped around my head, then started crying. I looked at Leo, unable to understand what was happening. This was not at all what was supposed to happen, and yet, it was. I was standing in my boyfriend's kitchen in an ancient Italian village, his mother hugging and kissing me while she cried happy tears for both myself and her own son. I was standing straight as a board when I finally started to come back into reality. Finally I dropped my bag and wrapped my arms around her and put my head on her shoulder. *What was happening?*

"Mamma," Leo said after about two minutes, as she was still not letting go of me.

"Sì?" she murmured to him in my chest.

"Penso che tu possa lasciarlo andare ora. Lo strozzeria," he chuckled, then she let go.

"I am so happy that you are here!" she said to me in perfect English as she pulled away.

I was too stunned to say anything. I was still processing what had just happened, but Leo looked at me and laughed. Joy and slight embarrassment infused me.

"I see that you have been using those English books I got for you," he said to her.

"Sì e ho fatto bene!" She walked towards him and pinched his cheeks.

"Landon, it is so nice to meet you. Leo has told me so much about you." She looked at me lovingly and back to her son, beaming.

"C'est tellement agréable de vous rencontrer aussi," I said to her in French.

She looked at Leo and winked at him. He laughed, and when he did it was a release of all the anxiety that he had built up since we left London. His face lit up and mother and son laughed together. These two had everything. The love between them was palpable and contagious.

"I made you dinner. You are tired after your fly, yeah?" his mother asked in French.

"We are. Thank you, mom," Leo said, smiling wearily.

That was the extent of my conversation with Leo's mother. I stayed a total of four days with them. During those days, we went wine tasting in the vineyards about three miles away and sat down for three full meals a day and a million cups of coffee and tea. The whole time, Mrs. Morreti was glued to her son. I could not understand what he was saying most of the time, but I knew that he was making her proud. I should have tried to speak more French to her, but I could not shake the feeling that in doing so I would be interrupting something sacred.

She watched everything he did and was so proud of each little thing. I, by no means, felt neglected because each time Isabella saw me, she came up to me and kissed me on both my cheeks. If not for the authenticity of the gesture, it would have bothered me. How could this woman love someone that she had just met? She kept giving and giving, and it was inexhaustible. Over those four days, I met Leo's cousins, who clearly were from the same bloodline. When Leo was showing his family his photos, his cousins squinted their eyes just like him. Then on the final day, after church and the café, when I began saying my goodbyes, Leo asked to take one picture of all of us together.

"I want to remember this moment. This is so pure that nothing in the world would be able to reframe it," he said to me as his family shuffled in around us. They all looked so happy that it actually made my heart hurt. I did not want to leave. I could not think of a time in my life when my family ever acted this way with each other. *It must be an Italian thing.*

"I will take it for you," I said to Leo, sticking out my hand.

"What? No, no, I think you are misunderstanding," he laughed to me. "You are what is going to solidify this memory. They all fell in love with you."

"Leo," I said nervously as I planted my feet next to him. A bubble of anxiety started in my stomach, and as it worked its way up my throat, I realized the feeling was guilt.

"Go on! Get in there." He pushed me towards the now-assembled group.

"Please let me take it. You deserve to be in there," I insisted, thinking of the day when Leo finds out I've been cheating and tears this picture apart– my lies made even more severe by my newly-established connection with his family.

"You know that I hate pictures, plus this is what I do. I know they want to remember this time together with you just as much as I do." He smiled, peering through the lens.

Then it dawned on me– this whole vacation was more painful than I could explain and more acute than anything I had experienced before. When I looked at his family gathered together, I saw the perfect unity. God was in Orvieto. I found myself obeying Leo's command and slowly walking toward the throng of outstretched arms waiting to welcome me into their circle. I turned my head and looked back at my boyfriend; I loved him. He gave me a thumbs-up before peeking his head behind the camera.

Isabella grabbed me and pushed me to the front line, squeezing me into her. The cousins in the back laughed with each other, the aunts and uncles kissed, arms wrapped securely around one another. This was a family. It was more than a group, more than a unit, more than anything I had ever experienced before. Leo may have left, but the strings which tethered him to this place and these people remained strong. Then Leo put up his hand and everyone got quiet. I was still looking around wanting to know how any of this was possible, feeling flushed with love and sadness. Isabella wrapped her arms around me, and before I was consciously aware of what I was doing, my head was on her shoulder as we squatted with each other in the front row.

Leo dropped his hand a second time, indicating that another picture had been taken, then did it again. In total, I was aware of three separate pictures, and as the group slowly dispersed down the tiny streets leading from the café back to their homes, I walked to Leo and gave him all the love I had for him. I was unaware of everyone and anyone around us; I wrapped both hands around his head and pulled him as close to me as possible. This was my choice, and he was part of that choice. As I slowly pulled myself out of his stupor, I was aware that all of his remaining family were smiling and cheering around us. It was one of those moments that I know will follow me to the grave.

Leo, thank you.

June

"How did it go? Did they pass you?" Sidonie asked me over the phone as I jammed the remaining clothes into my suitcases. My time in London had officially ended, and the city had given me more than I had ever hoped. I had mocked the kids who came back to the States saying that "abroad changed their life" but now could fully understand why this was so common. The only thing that would keep me from saying the same thing was my return. I didn't know when I would be back in Boston; I had already suspended my confirmation of attendance. I told admissions that I was going to "explore other educational options" as I attempted to discern what available transfers there were.

"They did," I said. "The instructor told me how impressive my speaking ability was and said that she had not seen an American with that kind of ability before. She said that I was probably even better than my girlfriend." I smirked.

"Shut up!" Sidonie laughed on the other end.

"Truthfully, they said that I did an amazing job and they are happy I am joining the team. You said that you will be able to help me move in when I arrive tomorrow?"

"I will be around all day," she said. I could hear the smile in her voice.

"Then I guess it is a date."

"I guess it is. I am so excited that you are going to be here for the summer. I know we are going to be working, but I have a lot planned for us. You might be sick of me by the time you have to go." Her voice dipped when she said the final words. It was the unspoken agreement; neither of us wanted to bring up the departure even though I had secretly already started to change my plans for senior year.

"I cannot wait," I said, imagining her bright eyes in front of me once again.

"Goodnight love, I am excited to see you tomorrow." She hung up the phone, and I sighed, feeling overwhelmed with every emotion.

After I returned from Italy with Leo, we had spoken more about what was going to happen this summer. He confirmed that he would be moving to Paris a week after me. He had to finish two jobs in London before he could start work in France. He also mentioned that his apartment was just fifteen minutes from mine. I didn't know how to feel because this meant that Sidonie, Leo, and I would be all located within twenty minutes from one another. The triangle was growing smaller. I still did not know who I was going to choose. That was a decision I was going to hold off for as long as possible. Already I was feeling the pressure and anxiety of somehow keeping them apart from each other. Desperately I wanted them both to remain in the dark while I took my good time pulling petals off flowers to determine who I loved more.

On that last day in London, I said goodbye to all my English friends and spent the afternoon with Jake. We went to the American Bar in the Savoy Hotel. It was one of the top-rated bars in the world, and it was how we both wanted to spend our last night together. After that, I departed and wished him good luck in Washington D.C. We were both incredibly excited with the opportunities that had presented themselves to us and were looking forward to senior year. I did not tell him that I was looking at universities in England. *This might be my last time seeing him for a few years*. But that was not important– what was important was that regardless of how often we talked, when I saw him next, we would pick up exactly where we left off. He was my best friend, and that was how things worked between us.

The move to Paris was incredibly easy. It was difficult lugging my three suitcases to and from the airport, but once I met Sidonie I knew that I had made the right choice. Each time I saw her she mesmerized me. The power of her physical and internal beauty was immense. My fairytale continued– that first day in Paris should have been projected onto the big screen. We had a picnic in front of the Eiffel Tower–baguette, pâté and cheese, red wine– while I waited for the landlord to finalize my three-month rental agreement. I surprised her by speaking in French for the entirety of the evening and before I knew it, I found myself straddling her in the bushes once everyone had cleared out for the evening. I knew that this would not be my everyday reality because my work schedule was ridiculous. We drunkenly walked around Paris until the landlord called and said that the apartment was ready. We made love in my bed and then she left. I was alone again, but this time I felt alive and invigorated. I was not concerned with anything but myself, and when I found myself drifting to either Sidonie or Leo, the memories of them calmed me. Love welled in me.

Just three days before I began at the embassy, Sidonie took me to Versailles because she had heard, I do not know from whom, that I had always wanted to go there. I was fascinated throughout the entirety of our visit and was enamored with the majesty of the old hunting palace. As I wandered through the great halls and pristine gardens, I imagined myself living there. I would have two dogs, but not the small dogs that the French were accustomed to; I would have two Doberman Pinschers – European not American. I would have kids. They would waddle around the halls until they learned to run. In

Versailles, I imagined my life, unencumbered by the minutia of reality. The only thing I could not visualize was who would be in the house with me. I saw my dogs, my kids, and even my siblings if they wanted to live in it, but I could not see Sidonie or Leo. I saw things that reminded me of their personalities, but I couldn't picture either of them in the palace. *All hypothetical, of course.*

Then came my first day at the French embassy. I could not have imagined a better first day. I was the only American citizen working with the communication team, and I knew that all the other interns, and even some of the department heads, were skeptical that I would be able to adequately fulfill the role. They started talking shit about me in French as if I couldn't understand them. Maybe they honestly thought I couldn't, so I smiled to myself before I opened my mouth and stunned them all. That was the first and last problem I had that day. Leo had prepared me well.

Those first few weeks in June were flawless, and I was happy. I was leading the intern team with strategy for diplomatic relations between France and the United States. Our President's frivolous comments did not help, but I kept reminding myself that at least I was not working on a way to reopen channels between the United States and Russia. My strategy and ideas were so unconventional, but also so effective, that I was personally introduced to the head of the communications team, a man called Bastien Thomas.

I was introduced to him at the very end of the third week, and that is when things changed. Bastien was a muscular 30-year-old man who was charming, but bullish, in every sense of the word. The first time I met him, my direct supervisor blushed throughout the entire conversation, and Bastien got so close to her that I wanted to excuse myself. That should have been my first warning. After she left, I was left alone in the room with him as he returned behind his desk.

"You are American, I see," he said in an accent, folding his arms casually and leaning against his desk.

"Yes, mais je peux parler couramment le française," I assured him in the best accent I could muster.

"I am sure English is easier for you," he said without looking at me.

"It is, but I can speak–"

"I just heard you. I will speak English," he snapped impatiently. "And you are doing good work in your department. That is why you are here right now?"

"I believe so," I said, suddenly feeling a little nervous.

He finally looked at me. I remember the moment so vividly because it caught me so off guard. When he finally raised his eyes to meet mine, it was like he was looking at a strange and beautiful animal. I saw the familiar swirl of lust that I have seen so many times before.

"Wow, handsome and smart. What do I have to do to get that?" He grinned a slanted, devilish sort of grin.

"Excuse me?" I said laughing, my face heating.

I laughed because I did not know what to say. The last thing I expected at the embassy was a scenario like this. He put my resume down on his table and moved in front of his desk.

"This is you, no?" He turned his computer monitor to me.

On his screen was the newest pictures from the Vogue shoot. It was me, half-naked, piled on top of three other guys. *My mother was singing 'I told you so' somewhere in the United States.*

"Yes, but I can explain," I stuttered, readjusting myself in my seat.

"There is no need. You must be either very lucky or very smart to have gotten a position here. My guess is that it is not luck. You would not be sitting here if it was." He smirked, his dark eyes closing in on me.

I laughed again, but this time it was strangled. He had not

stopped staring at me. Then he reached into his desk drawer and pulled out two glasses; that was my cue to leave.

"I, ah, don't drink," I said as I got up to leave.

"I doubt that." He pulled a bottle from his desk.

"Um, I am sorry for wasting your time Mr. Thomas. I don't really know why I was called here either. I should probably leave and get back to work now." I stood up and turned for the door.

"Stay seated. You just got here and I want to get to know this smart and handsome boy in my office." He poured whiskey into two glasses. Never in my life had anyone been this forward with me. I didn't know how to react. Although I felt incredibly uncomfortable, I didn't want to offend the man I was supposed to impress. He slid one of the glasses over to me and I sat back down.

"I really should be going. It's only 11 AM, so I probably shouldn't be drinking. It's against the rules of the internship program, I'm afraid." I flushed, feeling silly telling him what was and was not acceptable.

"Who do you think makes those rules? I grant you the ability to break the rule just this once." He winked at me. At that, my stomach turned over. I had only seen these types of situations on television, but I had never been in this position in real life before.

"Like I said, I don't really drink either." I pushed my glass back towards him. He did not like that.

His face stiffened. "Normally, in France, when someone offers you a drink, you drink it. It is *polite*," he said harshly, holding the bottle of whiskey with an iron grip.

I was confused and somewhat afraid, but I conceded and picked up the drink and took the first sip. I felt like I was on stage, he watched my every move so closely.

"Good. Your director said that you have some interesting ideas on ways to further open the communication channels between France and the United States. You know we are the United States Embassy, not the State Department."

"Yes," I sighed, in relief now that he was talking about the reason I was there. "I had a few ideas and I am well aware, but if this embassy could get on board then I think we could streamline–"

"How about you tell me over lunch then. Better yet, how about we go out to dinner?" he said, finishing his drink in one big gulp.

I started to fiddle with my hands, unable to believe how platitudinal his flirtations felt. It would have been funny if I weren't so uncomfortable, if it wasn't happening to me, if it wasn't *real*.

"Lunch or dinner? Don't you Americans like to make sure that your career is the best it could be? To get an offer for one-on-one time with the Director of Communication in an embassy would be very promising news for most Americans," he said slyly, glaring at me as if I were a plate of food. I can always tell in the way someone looks at me if they can see my humanness or not; I could see that to him I was something to rip apart, to own.

"Yes, well, I think that would be a good idea, but I just thought that I was here today to run a few ideas by you and then get your feedback. I don't think we need to spend an entire afternoon–"

"Or evening," he interjected.

"...over one simple idea. That would probably be a waste of your time," I said quickly.

"Do you like this job?" he asked out of nowhere.

"I do very much. I have learned a lot."

"You want to keep it?"

"Yes," I understood where he was going, and my heart dropped. A sour feeling like saltwater moved through my veins.

"Good. That is what I thought." He came towards me from behind his desk.

"It is very nice. I am sorry I...I might be reading this wrong."

"What?"

"This situation. I am sorry, but it is probably my fault. I just think that you ought to know that I am in a relationship with someone I like very much." I blushed, standing up from my chair so he was not towering over me. At this, his demeanor changed and he seemed to shrink in size. No longer was he looking at me like a piece of meat, instead, he was looking at me like I was a hurt animal.

"Yes. That is problematic. I am afraid you were misreading this situation. I simply wanted to know if you were willing to do what it takes to make a name for yourself. I guess I had the wrong opinion about you," he shrugged as he went back behind his desk.

"Should I go?" I asked, turning bright red.

"I think you should. Please tell your director that we had a good talk and that I will take your strategy as a suggestion."

"Okay, thank you." I quickly collected my things to go.

"However, if you change your mind about wanting to make something of yourself, you know where to find me."

"That I do," I said, already out the door. I slammed his office door in his face and then stood against the wall, collecting myself before returning to work. I was not going to tell anybody. I could not.

I saw Bastien every day for the remainder of my internship. If we were alone in the hallway, he would walk directly towards me, until the last minute, where he would laugh and move to the opposite side. He visited the interns in our department and offices on a regular basis so he could "check up on us", but he always spent more time in my cubicle than every other intern. A few of the interns spoke about the behavior but never said anything to me directly. I was grateful for the opportunity, but after the first three weeks the only thing getting me through the summer were the two people in the city with me.

Work took up much of my time, but on the weekends and weeknights I had figured out a system to see both Sidonie and Leo. With Leo's rising celebrity, it was not easy to find time to see him. I saw much less of him than I did in London because he was constantly working. That worked out for the best. Sidonie's job kept her busy as well, but she had more free time than Leo, so it made sense that I devoted more time to her. Every night that I saw her, I became more entranced with the woman in front of me. She showed me all the best holes-in-the-wall and we "did" Paris as it was supposed to be done. We went out, drank, danced, fell more in love, partied, socialized, had sex, and I got to know her so intimately that I felt empty without her.

The same was said for Leo when I was able to see him. We promised each other to separate work from pleasure and although my agents were angry that I had gotten a full-time job, they understood and made it work. During the week, I worked at the embassy and then on the weekend I would "work". It was by chance that I was booked for a shoot that Leo had also booked. Unlike Vogue, we did not have to keep our relationship a secret this time. It was obvious to everybody in the room that we loved each other. The photographs showed that even though he was not in them. The client loved the work so much that they wanted me to sign an exclusive deal with them. I had no control over that, and when my agents told me that they had passed on the offer, I did not fault them. *Someone loves me.*

When I was not with Sidonie or Leo, I wandered around Paris alone. It was peaceful and energizing at the same time. Trying to balance my relationships with work was beginning to take a toll, and although I was not ready to admit it to myself at the time, I knew a choice between the two was creeping up on me. I visited the statue of the lion and the gemsbok once a week when I went for lunch; I spent my whole hour sitting on a bench just staring at the intricacy. Paris was more than just the "City of Love"; to me it became the City of Life. The French took time out of their day to eat, sleep, spend time with loved ones, and art. During the month of June, I was quickly identified as the "smart intern" which did not bode well with my colleagues. I attempted to brush it off at first but then realized that it was not my fault.

I may have been given an advantage with the American work ethic, but I began to embrace my strengths without feeling guilty. It was the first time in my life I felt that way. I woke up, worked out, went to work, completed the necessary tasks, saw Sidonie or Leo or my colleagues for dinner and drinks, then would go home and fall asleep. Overall, it was a simple month and I was thrilled to have found myself. Then, on the last day of June, Sidonie dropped her bomb on me – the same one that Leo did.

"Landon, I need to ask you something," she said, her voice soft and hesitant.

"Anything babe," I said, looking up from my dinner plate. We were at my favorite restaurant and were about to go out afterwards. I felt unassailable between all the love I felt and the direction my career was heading.

"Do you know a lot of people here?" she asked, placing her silverware down on the table and zeroing her eyes in on me.

"What do you mean by that?" I said nonchalantly, though a tremor of nervousness was forming in my stomach.

"Do you have friends in Paris that I don't know about?"

"Well, I have introduced you to the people I work with, right? We went out with all of them last weekend when we met your friends."

"I know we did, but I am talking about anybody else."

"Can you be more specific?" I asked, biting the inside of my lip.

She sighed and then dropped her head.

"Sweetheart?" I asked, reaching my hand out toward hers.

"I know you are seeing someone else," she said with tears in her eyes. Then just like with Leo, my throat clenched and the dining room started to spin. My head rushed as I watched her beautiful face break in sorrow, her green eyes falling toward the floor.

"Why do you think that?" I asked softly. I knew she was just guessing because she did not retract her hand when I touched it.

"I don't know it. I just have a feeling." She wiped her face, sniffling.

"Babe," I said pulling myself closer to the table, "you are the only girl in my life."

Just like that, I pulled the same miserable stunt. I was deceiving another person I loved and was doing it easily. All through a lazy trick of language. Somehow this was still better than revealing the truth of myself to her– because if I did she might not love me anymore.

"I am not," she said through a heavy breath, staring up at me.

"What is causing this? Why are you saying this?" I asked in French.

"You just seem happy all the time," she said, then laughed at her own words.

I laughed back at her because it was a good thing; I was so used to people telling me the opposite.

"Is that a bad thing?" I asked.

"No," she laughed again, "I just know that people are not always happy. You are so happy with me and that is why I like you so much. Normal people are not always happy."

"You know that I am not normal, right?" I said jokingly, squeezing her hand.

"Oh yes, I know that." She sighed.

"Then what is it really?"

She hesitated a moment. "People talk about you."

"Come again?"

"People like you, a lot. They like you more than they like themselves. I am not like that," she said and then stopped.

"What does it matter what people say about me? If there is something you want me to work on or change, I will absolutely try for you." I flushed, focusing back on my food. I felt my face getting hot because other people's opinions still affected me.

"I am not like that. People like you a lot so I just don't see why that, tu sais, we are together." She looked directly at me, squinting slightly to see in my face if I understood her.

It was not the answer I was expecting because I saw her as the superior being, not me. Is that what she was even saying? How could someone as beautiful and contagious as her ever feel lesser than anybody?

"Babe, I love you so much," I said, and I saw her relax in response. Her eyes softened and she sat lower in her chair. "I don't know why that would make you think I was cheating on you with another girl. I don't know anyone in Paris, and all the other girls in my program are ugly."

"I know," she said through a choked sob.

"You do?" I said, trying to act surprised so I could change the mood.

"Yes. I saw them all last weekend and I thought I was prettier," she smile-cried.

"Well at least we know which one of us is humbler." I bounced my eyebrows which always made her laugh. Then she sighed again, wiping her cheeks.

"This is serious. I wanted to ask you. I just don't want to lose you."

Her final comment sobered me up. I kept trying to tell myself that a girl-guy romantic relationship was so different than a guy-guy relationship, but in reality they were all based around love. Although love took different forms, the principle did not. I was cheating on both Sidonie and Leo. I knew that. And though my love for both of them was full and true,

I knew it was not fair and that it would not sustain– that we were approaching the moment when both of them would discover the truth of who I was. I just didn't how to balance that powerful force that seemed to possess me, how to honor it. My heart sank and swelled when I looked at her– how tenderly she looked at me.

"I don't want to lose you, either. I promise that you are the only girl in my life. I really have enjoyed 'us' more than you could ever know – especially what we do at night," I said winking at her, trying to bring levity into the moment to avoid the approaching pain.

"Uh, gross, you are such an American boy." She smiled.

"I do love you. I am doing everything I can to show you that."

She paused and looked at me. She was trying to look into my soul to see if I was lying, but I had already opened and closed before she could get an accurate read. I reached across the table and grabbed her other hand, bringing it to my mouth. We spent the rest of dinner staring at each other from across the table. I loved her and did not want to lose her, but I was beginning to lose myself. Deep down, I knew that I would not change until forced to do so. I hated myself again, and there were no scapegoats available to me.

July: Part I

There were no other hiccups in my life after Sidonie asked me about any preexisting relationships. I saw her three nights a week and saw Leo the other three nights when his work lulled. Work had stagnated since I had met with Bastien and the projects were now being distributed to a beautiful blonde-haired girl who clearly was the dumbest one in the intern group. Her father had gotten her the job, and she could not tell you the difference between a media channel and a media matrix. All the interns, except myself, thought that this was strange, but after seeing her accompany Bastien out of the embassy late one night, I immediately understood what had happened. I had made my choice and would have to live with it, but I felt sorry for the girl. She was being coerced into a relationship that would certainly advance her career while simultaneously make her feel like shit.

At the beginning of July, Sidonie finally asked me to have dinner with her family. I had been wondering when the invite would come and although I was not very anxious to meet them, I was comforted when she asked. It was a beautiful summer night in mid-July and the entire intern cohort had been given the day off because there had been a previously planned visit by some powerful United States official. They told us that we had been working hard but that they needed our desk space for a reception area. None of us put up a fight, especially because our 12-hour days were becoming quite tiresome. It worked perfectly that Sidonie's dinner had been scheduled a week earlier. I had all day to sleep in, work out, walk through the park, then go over to her place. She said that she would text me the address of her family home, not her apartment, and that I was to be there at 2000 hours sharp. Her father was strict about the time, and I was incredibly interested to see how her family dynamic worked.

I had City Mapped the route and it suggested that I leave forty minutes prior. Sidonie told me that I should wear something nice – not a suit or a tux because her father hated people that always dressed like they were going to a ball – and a nice pair of pants. I was ready in plenty of time and then set off in search of the house. I took the metro to a bus station and then took that into a residential neighborhood. When she had first given me the address, I knew that it sounded familiar, but was not able to place where I had heard it before. Then, as I was stepping off the bus, I realized that this neighborhood was where all the diplomats and high-ranking officials lived.

The 16th Arrondissement was one of Paris's most influential and wealthy neighborhoods where some of the streets were literally lined with gold and silver. The townhouses were ornate, with any given one worth between 2-14 million Euros. I stared in amazement as I got off the bus and watched the luxury cars, rows and rows of them, drive past me. I followed the directions in my phone and when I found myself a block away, I encountered a guard booth. It was a gated neighborhood for the über wealthy. After handing over my license, he let me through the gate and I walked until I arrived at the house. To say that the house was a house would be a great understatement. This was a palace that happened to fit in between two other palaces. It was five stories high and covered in gold. There was the wrought iron balcony on the fourth floor with sparkling gold flakes embedded into the metal. The decorative mosaic on the first floor stretched around both sides of the house. When I knocked on the door, a butler greeted me and brought me into a reception area. I knew she came from money– but this was *entirely* different.

"Landon?" Sidonie's voice echoed through the hallway in front of me.

"Bonjour mon amour," I said back to her, trying to hide my astonishment. Usually rich people hated when you pointed out how rich they were. The butler gave me a sideways glance but I didn't care.

Then I saw her. She was dressed in the sexiest black dress I had ever seen her in. It was even more incredible than the one she brought to Madrid. It hugged her beautiful body tightly, her bare shoulders sensual and soft. When I kissed her, I wanted to stay in that position forever so that I could take in every aspect. I was disappointed when she pulled away, but it was obvious that she knew her effect on me.

"You are on time," she smiled, then glanced at the butler. That was his cue to walk away– he turned on his heel and returned to wherever corridor he came from in this massive estate.

"That was my only instruction so indeed I am. I hope I am not too early though. I thought that ten minutes early would be slightly too much ahead of schedule."

"This is perfect. I can give you a tour and then we'll sit down for dinner. My family is very excited to meet you," she said brightly, squeezing my hands.

The tour of the house was incomprehensible. The 17th-century artwork that hung in the hallways, the busts and sculptures in every room reminded me of Versailles. Sidonie had no idea the reality of where she lived. I wondered why I had never noticed her immense wealth before– maybe because she did not present herself in a manner that indicated she was incredibly rich. I wondered if she was embarrassed about it or just so used to it she didn't think to explicitly bring it up. She brought me to the library, the den, the multiple guest bedrooms, her room, the smoking chamber, the offices, the theater, and the other multi-purpose rooms in the home. As I walked through, I noticed that everything was ornate but barren. It did not look like anyone lived in the house even though I knew that she had younger siblings. It reminded me of what my house looked like growing up. It was beautiful, but it was not home. After she had pried me out of her room, we made our way to the living room where the table was perfectly set and the staff was waiting for us.

"My parents will be down soon," she said to me then yelled absently into the house, "Aceline...Patrik...il este l'heure du diner."

"I am surprised that you don't have people to call them," I said sarcastically, but she completely missed the snide remark.

"Please be polite. You are very polite with me, but my parents can sometimes be...difficult," she said sharply. She had the same anxiety Leo did– a new stiffness overcoming her.

"Yes ma'am," I nodded, looking towards the hallway where I heard small footsteps. Sidonie did not mention her family often, but I knew that she had a set of twins that were six years younger than her. When they burst into the kitchen, I was happy to see that they were normal. Not that I truly expected anything else, but normally when I see this much wealth there is always something wrong with the children.

"Hi there, I am Landon," I said in French after they had sat down in their designated seats. They did not say anything back; in fact, they would not take their eyes off me. I smiled awkwardly, not knowing what to do.

"Excuse me! How rude. Please say something back to our guest. He just spoke to you," Sidonie chastised her siblings.

"Hello," they said in creepy unison to me, reminding me

of the twins from *The Shining*.

"I am sorry. They aren't normally like this."

"Is that our special guest?" a voice said from down the hall.

Sometimes you know, based upon how certain people speak, how attractive they are before you meet them. This was Sidonie's mother. If I was not dating her daughter, I would have guessed that she was four or five years older than myself. She burst into the kitchen, wearing a red dress and high heels, then kissed both of her younger children on the head before rounding the table and kissing me on both cheeks.

"It is a pleasure to meet you, Ms. Mellac," I said to her in French, trying to control my blushing.

"The pleasure is all mine," she said in a smoky tone before taking her seat at the head of the table. She looked just as immaculate as her daughter. Beauty wore a strong gene in this family.

"Is daddy coming?" Sidonie asked.

"He said he will be right down and that we should start without him. He is finishing up a business call."

"Good!" Sidonie said, her face lighting up. She had spoken about her dad once or twice, but I could tell that he was obviously not involved in his children's lives.

We sat through the entire dinner. It was six courses and took three hours. Her father did not come, despite her mother asking the staff to rouse him from his study. The wine was excellent, the food was perfect, and the company was beautiful, but the conversation was boring and bland. Her mother and siblings only cared about my travels and my modeling. Not once did we stray from these business-oriented topics, but as I watched my girlfriend throughout the meal she did not indicate that anything was out of the ordinary. It must have been a common occurrence for her father to miss dinner. Not a word was spoken about his absence for the rest of the night.

Her siblings asked me what Sidonie was like with a boyfriend and why I liked her so much. She tried to shut them up but I said she had a beautiful soul and then I felt her hand find mine underneath the table. Her mother blushed when I said it, and by the way she looked at her daughter, I could tell she wanted that kind of love in her life. The night was majestic, in every sense of the word, but I felt empty when I left. When I kissed her afterwards, she did not seem fazed by the fact that the table was shrouded in silence for most of the meal. After we were all done, and we were all slightly drunk, I wished everyone goodbye as Sidonie walked me towards the door.

"Thank you for coming, my love. I had a wonderful night and I am so happy that you were able to meet my family. I have told them so much about you and I know that my mother will be talking about you to all her friends for the next week. I think the twins even liked you, which is an accomplishment in itself." She smiled.

"Do you want to come home with me tonight?" I said weakly after exiting the house.

"What?"

"Come home with me tonight. I will make us popcorn and I will open a bottle of red wine." I wanted to rescue her. I wanted to make her feel loved. The dinner I had just sat through was not love– it was formal and cold. There may have been brief exchanges of love at some points, but it was nothing like Leo's. I felt bad leaving her in the house alone. If I left now, it would feel like abandoning her to an empty house– to emptiness.

"I cannot. I told them that I would stay here tonight. I never stay here. That is why I got my own apartment."

"I will love you so hard tonight," I said winking at her and shaking my eyebrows.

"You are too drunk," she laughed.

"I am not. I just want to bring you home with me so you know how much I love you." I felt like a puppy pawing for a treat, but she didn't give in. She just laughed then kissed me goodnight. I had met her family and I told her that I had a great time, but I couldn't help but somehow feel a little sad for her as I walked away.

July: Part II

Two weeks after the family dinner, the French embassy invited everyone for an evening ball to honor a distinguished staff member who was retiring. They said that we could bring a plus one, and although I thought that the offer was a huge security risk for the embassy, I was not about to ask any questions. Sidonie was visiting her friend in Nice for the weekend and was unable to come, so I defaulted to Leo. He was thrilled, and we talked about what we should wear and how we were going to present ourselves throughout the night. He asked how he should introduce himself, but at that point I had given up trying to be someone I was not. It was too much energy, and I felt that to live a life like that I needed to be constantly on my guard. I told him that I would introduce him as my boyfriend. He liked that a lot.

Three hours before we were expected to show up, Leo and I got fitted for a tux by one of the designers he was working with. Leo must have mentioned that we were going to a gala and the designer quickly offered up his services. I originally doubted that any human could tailor two suits in three hours, but when I was presented with the silky black bag I knew it was going to be an interesting night. We had a great time getting dressed, then went out to dinner, and then proceeded to the embassy. Our transportation stood in a line thirty cars long and we waited for twenty minutes before we were let into the gates. The event planning team had done an extraordinary job, and the minute we entered the huge doors we were greeted with glasses of champagne and the smell of roses. It seemed that the theme must have been something to do with roses because there were jars, pots, pans, vases, and fountains filled with roses or rose petals.

In the main dining room, there was a massive rose bush resting in dirt. The whole night was mesmerizing, and three glasses of champagne in Leo and I were feeling good. I saw many of my colleagues, and they were shocked when I introduced Leo as my boyfriend. I saw it on their faces, but instead of being embarrassed I relished that fact that I was still able to surprise people. Dinner reminded me a lot of the first dinner that Leo and I had together and the mussels transported me back to DeChamorle's kitchen.

Feeling emboldened by the champagne in my system, I rose to dance with Leo when I

felt a strong hand grip my shoulder. I didn't immediately turn around because I assumed it was Bastien Thomas.

"Landon North?" a thick French voice boomed behind me.

"That is me," I said, turning around and immediately regretting the glasses of champagne. Better yet, Leo was returning with another one.

"I assume that you do not know who I am," the man said after I shook his hand. He was at least 6'4" tall with a neck that was almost as broad as his shoulders. He was clean-shaven and his hair was buzzed. He reminded me of an officer in the Army.

"I am quite sorry. I admit that I do not. I have only been working here for a few months and still do not know the people that I should," I apologized. By this point, Leo had caught my eye and gestured to help me but I curtly shook my head.

"My name is Rémy Mellac. I believe that you are dating my daughter," he said sternly.

The champagne bubbled in my stomach and gas escaped right into my cheeks. It was indigestion times a thousand. I couldn't find anything to say to him and immediately felt like I would collapse. My arms slackened, my head dropped, and my toes were tingling. I am sure that he could tell that I had been drinking, but I must have looked like I was going into some type of shock.

"Mr. Mellac," I stuttered, completely afraid of what was about to happen.

"I must apologize for missing the dinner my daughter planned the other night. I had a very important business call with some investors in California. It went much longer than I expected. My wife said that the food was cooked well, yes?"

"Oh yes, the food was exceptional," I stuttered, trying to conjure the color back into my face. "The duck and the caviar were some of the best I have ever eaten." I breathed heavily while my heartbeat echoed in my head, my temples pulsing wildly.

"I made sure that our favorite chef was there to prepare the meal. I am glad it was good. What are you doing here tonight? Up to no good?" he asked sternly. I couldn't tell if he was making a joke or not. I waited for a wink or an elbow jab but never received one.

"Yes, sir. I mean, no, sir. I work here and they invited all the interns for the dinner tonight. It has been lovely. I was going to ask Sidonie to come but she is away."

"Is she now? Who have you brought instead?" He looked over my shoulder to where Leo was sitting. I should not have turned around. I should have never turned around, but I did. I did turn around; Leo took that as a cue. I can't blame him— in fact, I can only thank him. He was quick to respond to what he thought was a cry for help.

"Landon, is everything okay?" Leo said to me.

Rémy looked taken back but a small smile had formed on his lips.

"Yes, Leo. Thank you. We are just finishing up so you can take a..."

"I am Leonardo. I am Landon's..."

"Photographer," I blurted out without hesitation. "Leo is a photographer and quite a good one at that. He has exhibits all over the world. Isn't that right, Leo?"

He looked at me wide-eyed for a moment then refocused his gaze back to Rémy. "Yes, but I was just going to say–"

"Actually, would you mind getting me a glass of water? Mr. Mellac and I are just finishing up, and then I think I should leave. I must have had too much champagne," I said, attempting to laugh at myself. Neither man thought it was remotely funny. I wanted to disappear.

"Is there anything else I can get you?" Leo spat as he walked away. "Would you like your picture taken before you go as well?"

"I am sorry about that," I said to Mr. Mellac, who was intently studying me. His gaze was hard and unreadable. I couldn't have invented a more humiliating moment if I were the biggest masochist in the world.

"There is no need," he said slowly. "I have worked with creative types before and understand how difficult it is to deal with them. It is very kind that you brought him here tonight. He would never have this opportunity without you. He should be more grateful."

"It was nice to meet you, Mr. Mellac. I apologize, but I am feeling quite sick and was just about to head out before you caught me. I hope that I will see you soon," I said quickly, collecting my coat from the back of the chair.

I didn't bother to look back at Rémy because I could feel his eyes following me all the way to the door. Leo was already waiting with a glass of water, but he was furious. I saw it on his face. His jaw clenched and squared out like it always did when he was pissed. Here we were taking turns hurting each other in front of other people. Supposedly important people that we wanted to impress– apparently more important than our relationship and the love between us.

"What was that about?" he asked angrily. "I thought we had a deal coming to this thing. You introduced me as your boyfriend to everyone else, but for that man you said that I was your photographer like I was your personal bitch." His eyes seared into mine. It was always impossible to escape that confrontation.

"It was not like that. I don't know why I said it. I just thought that older people have a harder time with the whole gay thing and he was an important businessman so I didn't want to ruin any chances with him."

"I see. Oh yes, you did not want to ruin any chances to climb the ladder. I understand," he scoffed.

"Leo, look, I am sorry. That was not how I should have acted, but I understand if you are hurt." I gently put my hands on his arm, but he flicked me away.

"*If* I am hurt? *If* I am hurt? I am hurt. You just diminished our relationship with one word. Tell me how I wouldn't be hurt by that," he almost shouted. Neither of us were in the right mindset for this.

"Can we talk about this outside?" We walked toward the entrance. "If you would just listen to me–"

"No. I am not going to listen to you because you obviously do not take any of my feelings into consideration. Remember that it was *me* who got you this job, so don't try to say that I am the one who has a problem."

"Leo…"

"No. Actually, I think I am going back to my apartment tonight." He stormed out the front door.

"How is this any different from when you ignored me at the Vogue shoot? You pretended like you couldn't even remember my name!" I seethed.

"Do *not* play the victim! I told you that was what had to happen so we could both benefit. I also got you that job. *I* opened up that door for you and now you repay me with pretending like I am your *cagna*," he spat, raising one hand towards the doorman so that he could signal for a cab.

"Leo, wait, please don't go. Can we just talk this out right now, please?" I pleaded as I scrambled to push the effects of the alcohol out of my brain.

"No. I played along, again, with whatever happened back there. Now you have to play along when I say that I want a break." He walked towards the cab. He was just one person, but as he walked to the cab, I knew that I was losing part of my world. Suddenly he felt so remote from me, impossible to reach. "I will call you when I am ready to speak again. I need to figure out how I want to proceed." He sank into the backseat and closed the door without looking at me again.

I stood there for twenty minutes while I replayed the night in my head. I was forced to say that to Mr. Mellac. If I did not, then I would have lost someone that I loved. *I did lose someone that I loved.* Leo was gone. *That happened so quickly. Our entire relationship just changed with one introduction. We were done?* But if I admitted to Rémy that he was my boyfriend then I would have to then explain what I was doing dating his daughter. It was a catch-22, and either way I was bound to lose, but it was a moment I knew was coming– a moment I had been setting myself up for since I saw both of them for the first time. I was tempted to go back into the party to either make a bigger ass of myself or to pretend nothing just happened, but I decided against it and signaled for the doorman to call me a cab as well.

The minute I got back home I called Sidonie and acted like everything was okay. I told her that I had met her father and she was overjoyed. She asked me how it went and I told her that he seemed to like me. She asked me how the party was and asked who I brought. I told her. I told her that I brought a close personal friend, a photographer that I had met in London who was now working in Paris. At first, she did not say anything, but then she chirped how nice it was to have given him the opportunity to mingle with all the "important people" in the world. We ended the call on that note.

That last week of July was hell. Leo stood his ground and did not text or call a single time. He had slipped through my fingers so quickly that I believed I had imagined the entire party. I saw Sidonie twice. She told me that she had talked to her father, but I could tell that he had said something to her that made her uneasy.

"And?" I asked, grappling for any hint that would show the truth behind their conversation. We had ordered gelato and were walking down a side street towards her apartment.

"Landon, I do not know. He was probably just preoccupied. He said you were very handsome."

"Sidonie, did I say something?"

"This is not even anything you should be worried about. Listen to me, he is just hard to…talk to. He is always so busy with his business that his conversations are short. I would not take it personally."

"Do you understand that I do not even know what to take personally because you are not saying anything of substance to me. Did I not make a good first impression?"

"Landon," She sighed.

"No, I am serious. Tell me. What did he say?"

"He has never liked anyone…"

"Sidonie! Tell me. What did he say?" I shouted at her in the middle of the sidewalk. It was the first time I had ever raised my voice in her presence and it caught her off guard. *It worked, it got the job done.*

"He just said that you seemed preoccupied. That is why I am telling you,"

"That is not all. I know when you are holding back on me. What else did he say?" I questioned, rubbing my hands on my head. *I forgot to say sorry for shouting, I forgot.*

She paused, avoiding eye contact. When she picked her head up and brushed away the three locks of hair that had fallen in front of her eyes, they were glimmering.

"He said that you were not what he expected." She sighed again. She was telling the truth but there was just a little bit more to go.

"What does that mean? What did he expect?"

"This is probably a reflection on me. My other boyfriends, they were very rich and very...I do not know. He did not say that he did not like you because you are not rich. We are so young, he does not expect you to be from wealth, my other boyfriends...they all came from the same neighborhood. He just said he thought you would be more like them."

"Them, meaning your previous boyfriends?"

"Yes."

"Can you tell me anymore?" I asked but I was still missing the point. Why was it so hard for her to have told me that from the get-go?

A sigh and another glance away from me.

"He...he said that you seemed, uh, you seemed, how do you say this in English? He said you seemed unsure." She spitted and I almost laughed. *Why was this so difficult?*

"Unsure in what way?"

"Unsure about yourself. I do not know. He did not say anymore."

"Oh, okay, I do not really know what to say about that." I asked but she still would not meet my eyes.

"Something about the photographer," She whispered as she continued walking down the sidewalk.

"The photographer?" I asked but the words got stuck in my throat.

I knew what Remy probably said to his daughter. *It all made sense.* Chances were, if he showed up at the party, he knew other people at the party. I had been introducing Leo as my boyfriend all night. Not only was he at the party but he sought me out. Either my name had come up in conversation between him and someone else or he recognized me from a random picture his daughter had shown him.

"Yes. The photographer."

"What did he say about the photographer?"

"He said the photographer seemed protective, of you. He did not like that. That is why I am telling you; it is less a poor reflection of you. I think the circumstance could have been better, that is why I wanted to introduce you at our house but it is his fault that he did not make dinner. Do we really have to continue talking about this? I do not want to talk about this anymore."

"Sidonie," I said grabbing her sticky, gelato-coated hand. My hands were sweating so profusely that had it not been for the ice cream, she would have felt the dampness. "Are you telling me he did not say any more than that?"

"Yes," *That was it. She was being honest.* "That was all. Can we just eat our gelato in peace? I want to go home and watch a movie with you." She didn't look at me the same way, nor was she as open or carefree. Something had shifted, and in a big way.

In the back of my mind, I began to realize that this was either the beginning to an end or simply the end.

First week of August

I was alone again. This time it was the unbearable type of loneliness. I was well aware that I was doing it to myself. There was no one else to blame. I was back to what I was used to. It was the same feeling that had haunted me before I met either one of the people who I now valued above all else. As I ambled aimlessly through my vault of memories, starting to sift through times in my life when I felt content, I stumbled upon one from when I was in eighth grade.

My family and I were in Jackson Hole, Wyoming on a sightseeing tour of western America for my spring break. I was thirteen years old, Colman was eleven, Molly was ten, and Kendall was nine. We were the North Four. It felt good to think about the North Four again – the unit that was going to work together to build a dynasty. We had just landed in Jackson Hole Airport. As the plane dipped back beneath the clouds, the pilot of the single-engine aircraft spoke through the intercom and told us to look out the windows; we were not only descending through the clouds but seemingly brushing the tips of mountains.

The snow-tipped peaks of the Teton Mountains were so unreal that I kept pinching myself. The massive bodies of the mountains, spread out beneath the wingtips, had such substance to them that the ridge looked as if it stretched forever.

Then the plane shuttered and we lost altitude quickly. If I had been looking at my water, I would have seen it hover in mid-air before splashing back into my cup. I reached over and clung to my mom's arm because I thought that we were for sure going to dive into a freefall. That didn't happen, and after the pilot apologized for the turbulence, I pressed my face back against the window of the small plane.

The rest of the descent was easy and the plane touched down on the single runway with ease. There was no terminal bridge in that airport so we had to walk down the steps of a pull-away staircase. When I took those first steps into that chilled Wyoming air, I felt happy. I was not overjoyed, I was not sad, I was not even neutral to be there. It was the type of happiness that I have only felt on rare occasion like under the Northern Lights in Iceland, all alone in the Sahara Desert, or when I ran along the railroad tracks in my hometown, my two dogs in front of me.

This type of happiness, I cannot be classified as happiness because it is something more and something less. It did not wash over me like a tidal wave, as a great release of energy, and did not seep into me. It bubbled from inside of me– not like a spring or a volcanic eruption, rather it filled my entire body as if my insides had rearranged themselves. The aching euphoria that greeted me as I stepped into the valley between the Teton Mountains was not overwhelming, but it did complete me. In that moment, standing on top of the pull-away stairs, as the baggage carts drove towards the stopped plane sitting on the single runway of an airport in the middle of nowhere, I was a human being as large and as small as every other human being.

I was standing in that same spot as many people before me. My family was coming out with their carry-ons and empty water bottles, to stand where I was standing, to see what I was seeing. I had nothing to worry about and everything to hope for. I was great because I was small. I did not have to live up to the expectations of the mountains that towered behind me or strain to fight against the wind that had just had destroyed the stewardess' hair. The mountains and the winds had already claimed those expectations. There was a serenity that accompanied the wholesomeness of that Jackson Hole air. As I sat in my apartment in Paris, the memory brought a momentary reprieve. I was alive, and no one else was in control of that feeling but me.

"Landon." It had been two weeks since Leo contacted me.

"Oh my God, Leo, I have missed you so much," I whimpered into the phone during my lunch break, straining not to cry at the sound of his voice.

"That is what I am calling about. I think we should meet and go over some things. Are you going back to the States on the 22nd still?" he asked.

"We can talk about that, too," I said hopefully. I had not been given the chance to tell him that my credits from Boston College were approved for transfer at Oxford. I would have to spend another year in study, but my three previous years at Boston College would not have been for nothing.

"Can you meet–"

"Yes," I interjected.

"You did not even hear when I was going to ask."

"I don't care. Tell me when works for you and I will meet you," I said anxiously, wondering what he looked like now– if his scruff was still the same length, his hairstyle the same.

"I will meet you at the west entrance of Parc du Buttes-Chaumont. I know it is far from you but–"

"I don't care. I will see you there at?"

"7 PM."

"I will be there right on the dot."

He paused on the other, end and I immediately thought that the overt affection was too much. I was embarrassed but desperate and didn't care if I had to make a fool of myself to get him back.

"I will see you in a few hours," he said solemnly then hung up.

Like magic, which I should have taken as another sign, Sidonie called an hour after I had hung up with Leo.

"Landon."

"Sweetheart." My heart raced, hot blood sweeping through my body.

"Can we talk?"

"Yes, is everything okay?" I asked nervously.

"Everything is fine. I know that I have been moody lately, but I want to apologize to you. You did not do anything wrong, but I often overthink things and know that you are trying your best to make me feel happy. I would love to see you."

"How does tomorrow sound?" I asked, trotting through the metal detector into the embassy.

"Tomorrow is perfect. You are off work?"

"They have not made me come in on a Sunday yet, so I'm hoping they don't make us start now," I joked, though my heart felt heavy.

"Then I will see you tomorrow. I want to take you to one of my favorite restaurants."

"Perfect." I smiled like an idiot then jumped into the cab and waved thank you to the security guard at the gate.

Leo arrived at 1900 precisely. I watched him from my spot on the bench as he looked around until he found me. He strolled over to me, not breaking eye contact as he walked. He looked extremely intimidating – exactly like the first day I met him. Were we about to start over?

"Bonjour," he said, and I smiled back at him. He was carrying a folder with a stack of paper in it. "I have been thinking a lot about what happened two weeks ago, and I admit that I overreacted. However, I do know that I am not to blame for how the fight started. It is only my reaction that I am apologizing for."

I stayed silent so there were no grounds where he could say I was not listening.

"Are you going to say something back?" he said after some silence, looking at me intently.

"I am sorry as well. It was very immature of me to put you in that position. I know that regardless of where I am or who I am with, that it is only the environment that changes, not me. I should have introduced you as my boyfriend because I am very proud of that."

He looked surprised at my response.

"Now, are you going to say something?" I joked.

"Yes. I will say that I missed you very much." He put his hand on mine. Warmth spread up my arms. He noticed my reaction because he scooted closer to me and rested his head on my shoulder. We stayed in that position until it started to get dark and we did not say a single word. There was nothing else to be said and nothing else to be done. What we did for those forty minutes was enough for the both of us.

"I am afraid that I must move onto the business side of things now," he said eventually, running his fingers along my goosebumps.

"I was wondering what was in the folder," I said, snatching it out of his hand. It was photos of me – just me. I was everywhere. I was in his apartment in London, the first time we met. Then I was in Hyde Park. Then I was in Blanchette. Then I was in a studio. Then I was on a sidewalk looking back at him. Then I was in Paris. Then I was in Orvieto sitting next to his mother reading a book. Then I was sitting across from him at a dinner table in our favorite café.

"This is my exhibit– well, this is my *main* exhibit. I am forced to add more editorial-esque body shapes so I can impress the creative directors that are coming, but you are my main exhibit on the 13th."

Blinking and breathing became laborsome. My face was everywhere, but I looked so different in every picture. I could not recognize myself. Is this how he saw me? So many sides of myself I did not realize existed.

"If you don't like them, I don't have to use all of them," he said nervously. I could not respond to him because I was fixated on the pictures, and I found myself only able to process one thing at a time. "Shit, I knew I should not have submitted them without asking you first. Even if you don't like them, could you do me just this one favor and sign the slip? I am so sorry that I did not ask you first, but if you can do me this one favor by signing off on them then I promise I will repay you."

He was amazing – truly amazing. I snapped the folder shut and kissed him with more emotion than I had ever kissed anyone in my life before. It was liberating because I was allowing myself to feel this way, yet, also constraining because I was slowly making the decision to end things with Sidonie. I did not realize this at the time– it only came afterwards when I replayed the memory of us on that bench in that park.

"…which is why I wanted to apologize to you," she told me a day later.

"There is no problem here. I just wanted to make sure you were okay."

"I am now," she smiled, gently rubbing my chin with her fingers.

We had spent that afternoon walking through the park in practically our bathing suits. It was 90 degrees and sunny. Leo had told me that although we had just gotten back together, he had to work non-stop until the exhibit was over. Sidonie and I went to lunch, got ice cream, and she apologized for treating me as she did. I couldn't understand what was wrong with me, but the conclusion I came to at the time was that I loved both of them too much and I needed just a little more time. Things reverted back to normal between her and I.

The things I value in memories are not the *feelings* that accompany the multitude of external factors that help differentiate a moment from another. The thing about memories, that make it possible to remember them in the first place, is the solitude that each one brings– this is why all memories are different. My brother, who stepped out of that plane after me, does not remember the turbulence of the air causing the plane's engine to momentarily stall. How can I know what he remembers as he stepped onto those metal steps of the roll-away staircase, looking at the flat plains and steep mountains that surrounded us? The solitude of memory is collaborative and isolating at the same time. Part of my Jackson Hole whole-someness is because my family was there with me.

Those social relationships that I deeply valued influenced my outlook of the surroundings when I exited the plane. I sat in my Paris apartment thinking about each memory that I held dearly, that showed me something different about my-self – showed me who I truly was and what I was meant to be doing. What I had spent my time doing over the past twenty years of my life had been full of distractions, meaningless dead-ends, empty principles– yet it was not for nothing. The path to a fulfilling and meaningful life is not a straight shot; it is winding and recursive, meandering and blurry– a path that even in its confusion led me to connect with new people, find new passions, discover what did not settle well in my soul.

Second week of August

Leo's show was in the European House of Photography, and the night before his opening he told me that he wanted me there to organize the photographs with him. I had no idea why he wanted my help because it was his show and his vision. Nevertheless, I obliged because I had not seen him in almost a week; I was willing to do anything to be with him. I arrived at his exhibit five hours before the opening, unsure if I was supposed to dress up or if he wanted me in regular clothes.

"Hello handsome," he said, kissing me on the cheek. His assistants and maintenance crew flittered about the gallery, gawking at me. My face was plastered everywhere.

"It looks great in here." I peered around, finding my reflection everywhere. *To be clear, I was not the only subject but I was the majority.* Each room seemed to have a different theme. The one we were standing in looked like a room straight out of Versailles. This was the room attributed to the more editorial photos that he had taken of the other models. I did not want to touch anything because it was so daintily decorated; anything could break at moment's notice. He was incredibly talented. Splashed across the velvet walls were impeccable images of men and women in the nude, contorted in so many different but beautiful ways, almost as if they were trying to mimic certain animals.

"Did you see the other rooms as you walked in?" he asked hopefully.

"I did. I can go work in there if that's what you need me to do."

"I'll come join you. I need your honest opinion in here though. I wanted to get this done first so I could focus on the more important subject in the others." He smirked.

"Funny," I said, but really I was honored with the compliment. "I don't know if I could offer you any advice that you do not already know. It looks incredible in here and I mean it. The only suggestion I have would be to add maybe a single flower beneath each picture. I know it's random, but all these people take such different shapes that if you picked a flower that somewhat reflected the mood of the photo, I think it would be just an additional touch."

"Amazing," he muttered to himself as he surveyed the room. "I think I will do that. That is extremely random, but it would add a…je ne sais quoi to the room. I think it would work nicely. Hold on, I will be right back."

Walking over to a group of three women who were pointing at different spots on the wall, obviously critiquing his work, he relayed my suggestion. They smiled and nodded, then one of the women got on her phone. The nude pictures were not huge but were the size of regular photographs. Compared to the other rooms where my face was 100 times larger than my body, it was a welcomed change. I strolled along the walls, briefly skimming my fingers over the velvet, looking intently at each picture. The first one was the picture that Leo had showed me in his apartment; it was the picture of the male ballet dancer. I smiled to myself because it seemed like only yesterday that he was trying to intimidate me.

Next there was a pregnant woman, completely naked, holding barbed wire. The symbolism was too complex for me to handle because even when I thought about it, I couldn't decipher what it was meant to say. There was the backside of a naked boy, the silhouette of a fat woman, and even a set of naked twins who looked nothing like each other from the neck down. The room was very eclectic, and I knew it would earn Leo the big points with the creative directors.

"I told them your idea and they loved it." Leo came over to me where I was observing the naked twins.

"I'm glad I could help. Can I do anything? Do you need help hanging the pictures or setting up the water? Also, what should I wear tonight? You obviously seem ready to go, but I have only been to two art exhibits before and I wore jeans and a sweatshirt to both of them."

"Then you can wear that here," he said happily, pinching my arm.

"Leo, you are in a tux. Tell me what I should wear, not what you think I want to wear."

"Fine, if you put on a button-down and a nice pair of jeans that will be fine. I don't exactly know how many people are coming tonight, so don't get your hopes up."

"Too late. This is all about me so my hopes are already up," I said jokingly.

"Funny American boy. You have so much to learn. But if you do want to help then you can go into one of the other rooms and ask if my assistants need any of your services," he said, becoming distracted by something behind me. "I will see you later." He kissed me on the lips before walking towards a set of workers hanging up another picture of me. "It starts at 7 PM, but you can come back at any time. I have to go tell these idiots the importance of that picture."

I left the velvet room and proceeded to do exactly as he directed, but no one needed any help at all. Everybody seemed on top of their work so I took the time to stroll around the rooms. There was a room that looked like: a WWII bunker, a meadow in Northern Italy, New York City, a white room, and then a room made entirely out of wood. I did not understand if there was an overarching theme, but because most of the photographs had not been mounted yet, I couldn't invest any more time. I left.

Three hours later, I was dressed and ready for the night. Although this was Leo's night and he was the one who should be nervous, I was also nervous because my face was 75% of the gallery. Did I really make that much of an impact on him that I deserved a night dedicated to his work? I didn't think so, but he must have thought opposite. From the time I left to the time I returned, the hall looked completely different.

Then people started to arrive. They did not arrive one-by-one; they arrived in masses. I was completely blown away by the initial turnout. An hour into the opening, there was a dip and I thought that it was practically over. I was wrong. It seemed like a thousand more people arrived each proceeding hour, and at 2200, the entire exhibit was packed with people and glasses of champagne clinked in merry symphony. I wandered around and introduced myself to those people whom Leo had deemed important enough for me to meet. Each and every person I met commented on the strong relationship that Leo and I must have. To say the least, the night was more than either of us could had hoped for.

Then it happened. My finale; the beginning of the end.

Sidonie showed up.

I was standing in the back corner of the front room, talking to a creative director from an up-and-coming fashion line when I saw her head through an opening in the crowd. The plastic cup broke in my hand. I apologized to the woman and told her that I had to go clean it up. I slipped along the outskirts of the different groups that were gathering at each picture and then found myself staring face to face with the girl I had fallen in love with. I needed to get her out.

"Sidonie?" I said, trying my best to sound calmly surprised.

"Landon, oh my God! How come you did not tell me that this was happening tonight?" she said, completely bewildered. She did not seem angry that I had not told her – or suspicious. She was simply excited to be there with me.

"I was told kind of last minute actually. That photographer from London, that I took to the ball a few weeks ago? Well, he just told me that I was going to be his exhibit. How funny is that?" I said as I guided her closer toward the door.

"How do you think I found out about it?" she laughed.

"What do you mean?" I asked, trying not to get nervous.

"My father was the one who said that I should come tonight! Don't tell anyone, but he donated a few thousand Euros to the gallery. After he met you at the party, he looked up the photographer you were with and he said his pictures were exceptional. He wanted to carry the show from the sidelines." She smiled brightly, her face so full of love.

I felt the corners of my eye twitch. This was not a coincidence that her father told her to attend. He was the only one in Europe who had me pegged without my own disclosure. We had spoken only a few sentences but her father nailed it. He saw me and he was protecting his daughter. *He loves her after all.* He had also created the perfect situation for me to squirm under. This was his test. Perfectly orchestrated humiliation– unless I could somehow avoid the inevitable crash-collision that was bound to happen any minute now.

"I had no idea you had such a close relationship with him!" She stared up at the pictures adoringly, her red mouth slightly agape.

"Yes, it really has been quite the summer as you know, but I was just about to leave. Would you like to come back with me?" I asked quickly, feeling my anxiety rising.

"I just got here. Come show me the rest of the pictures!" she said excitedly.

"They really aren't anything much different. How about

this– what if we go back and we celebrate by opening a bottle of wine and watching a movie or something? I have been here for such a long time that I was just about to leave anyways." I repeated, panicking and trying to gauge her reaction. My eye was twitching like a live wire, my pulse thumping wildly, as I tried to pull her toward the door. The unadulterated panic felt as though a live wire had been surgically implanted in every cell in my body.

"Come on, this is a big night for you." She squirmed out of my grip. "At least show me the other rooms, and then we can leave. I want to see all the different moods of Mr. Landon North." She smiled then turned away, walking towards the middle of the room.

"Okay, but let's make it quick. I don't feel that good either."

"Absolutely, my love." She stood on her toes to kiss me on the cheek. "Lead the way!"

I scanned the crowd through every single room. I knew Leo would be anchored in the velvet room, so I steered clear us clear from that area. I rushed her through each of the five rooms and finally felt a calmness wash over me as I eyed the door. Maybe I'd make it out unscathed after all. I looked at Sidonie and motioned toward the door with my head, when suddenly a hand grabbed mine through a group of people.

"Leo," I said breathlessly, my face exsanguinated of all color in an instant. My hands began to shake so badly I had to shove them in my pockets. Little sparks floated through my vision. The dreaded moment of my worst fantasy had finally come to fruition.

"I've been looking for you all over. I wanted to introduce you to a few more people. Now, I know what you are going to say– that you have met so many people already– but I think these people could really help you," he said excitedly, squeez-ing my hand.

I couldn't respond to him because my other hand was then

grabbed by a more delicate bone structure.

"Landon," Sidonie said to me and, again, I couldn't respond to her.

I looked between the two of them as my vision started to turn black around the corners. This was going to happen eventually, and I had lost the choice to make it happen on my own time. I set myself up for this moment since the very beginning. How could I have been so stupid? *I was a coward.*

"Hi," Leo said happily to Sidonie after it was obvious that I was not going to introduce them.

"Hi. You must be the genius who put all of this together. I must tell you how incredible everything was tonight. I am blown away." She shook his hand, smiling, touching my arm.

"Who are you?" Leo said, and I heard the first words of suspicion seep into his voice. I was screaming at myself from inside my head, but I could not find the words. I felt like Alex in *A Clockwork Orange* during his rehabilitation– my eyes forced to witness the terror around me, my body unable to do anything to prevent it. I was the one to place myself in such a helpless position, and now I was too shocked to worm my way out of it.

"I am so sorry," Sidonie said looking at me weirdly, "I am Sidonie Mellac. I am Landon's girlfriend. I am so sorry that we have never met before, especially because you two seem to know each other so well."

I stood fixated on the picture of me from the day at Brighton beach, completely shrouded in pure joy, coming out of the water flipping the camera off as I did so. How fitting that all of this was going to happen right here and right now. I was literally face-to-face with myself, saying 'Fuck you' to me. How fitting this was– standing in the middle of two people that I loved, two people who knew nothing about each other.

"Excuse me?" Leo said to her in complete shock. *First shock, then anguish.* She noticed it immediately and looked at me, trying to get me to say something. I vaguely remember her squeezing my hand trying to bring me back to life, but I needed a full revival, not a hand squeeze.

"I am Landon's girlfriend, Sidonie."

He did not miss a beat this time. The anguish evaporated as the color seeped from his face but somehow, *somehow*, he found the strength. It was I had fallen in love with. The pure selflessness, his strength.

"It, yes, uh, it is an absolute honor to meet you. I am so sorry that I did not understand you the first time. I am Italian, so it takes me longer to process things in English. Yes, of course I know who you are. What an honor to meet such a beautiful... woman. Landon," Leo beamed, and for a moment I thought he had completely misunderstood what she had said. Then when he looked at me, right in the eyes, the gateway to my soul, the soul currently undergoing a lockdown, I knew that he had not misheard or misunderstood. I had made it over the finish line. I was not close to the end anymore, I had finished. In a way, it was the worst thing to ever happen to me but also one of the best. I was not allowed to hide anymore to those I loved.

"Please do not apologize. I'm sure that you've been speaking to people all night. I just wanted to introduce myself and thank you for giving Paris such an incredible exhibit. I am so pleased that I could have made it."

"I am so glad that you were able to come. Please, excuse me, I must continue making the rounds," Leo said joyfully, letting my hand drop to my side.

"He seems so nice. I am shocked that you have not ever talked about him." She was completely oblivious to what was actually happening. "I think I have seen everything now if you want to go home, my love."

I just shook my head and let her lead me towards the door. I finally found my voice in the cab ride home and told her that I was coming down with the flu. She offered to take me back to my apartment to take care of me, but I declined and said that I just wanted to go to bed.

"I am so glad that I was able to see you tonight. People could not get over how wonderful you are. I am even more glad that you are mine. I love you. Please feel better." She stepped back into the cab. I watched her drive away, but then immediately called another cab to bring me back to the gallery. I had no idea what I was doing. I was given countless chances and I took none of them. The second cab dropped me back off at the gallery and people streamed out of the building because the exhibit was now closing.

It was a drastic change when I reentered the building – poetic justice. When I got there this afternoon, before all the people came, the exhibit was spotless and pristine just like my life. I had everything I had ever dreamed of; I was the selfish center of my own world and also of those around me. *They had paid to see me only because of Leo. He provided me the one-in-a-lifetime chance. And I repaid him by?* Now, walking back into the building, there were empty champagne glasses on the floor, garbage everywhere, and it was empty of everything that had previously given it life. The only things which remained untouched were the photographs and the flowers, which were beginning to droop. It was eerie to walk back in because other than the crews assembled to clean the garbage off the floors, there was a single soul left in the gallery.

He was standing all alone looking at the exact picture that I was looking at when Sidonie introduced herself to him. I couldn't cry, I couldn't smile, I couldn't charm anyone anymore because there was nothing left to charm - everything was out in the open.

"We are closed," he said when he heard my footsteps echoing across the granite floor. When I did not stop, he said it again and started to turn but I got to his side and he knew who I was. I had no right to say anything to him. *I had just delegitimized our memories, we now knew that I was a liar. He would never believe how real it was to me.* I stood, shoulder to shoulder, and stared at the picture. That sad thing was that I did not even remember the moment when he took the photograph. *He did, it was enough for him to enlarge 300 times its original size. He brought the memory back to life.* I remembered the day, and the beach. I must have noticed him taking a picture of me or my middle finger would not have been up, mocking him. *Mocking me.* He was wearing that pink bathing suit, the one he miraculously found on the boardwalk as I dealt with the fact that I would not be getting a tattoo.

In the picture, the sand umbrellas lined either side of the frame, almost symmetrically, but there was an open stretch of beach as I clambered out of the water. I was not flexing, but he captured the moment in a way that I could see all the finer muscles in my body that were usually photoshopped into oblivion during post-production. My smile, a smile that I had only seen through his lens, completely contrasted the symbolic gesture of the middle finger. My teeth were open to reveal a small part of my tongue, and my one of my legs was back as I tried to regain balance after coming out of the waves. I could not imagine what he must have thought taking the picture, but now we were staring at it as both of our known identities were flicked off.

"She is beautiful," Leo said when the maintenance workers shut the door to the other room to begin vacuuming.

"She is," was all I could say after the five-minute period of silence.

"I believed you when you said I was the only one because you were telling the truth. I could tell," he said softly, and I could tell that he was holding back tears. His reaction triggered the tears in mine, "Then, I replayed the words you said to me, over and over again, in my mind, because I felt so stupid for believing you. It took me until ten minutes ago to realize that you were completely honest with me. I was the only *guy* in your life, wasn't I? Those were the words you said; it was not "only one in your life", it was "only guy in your life". That was true. I don't even need to ask you if that is still true. I know so."

"I didn't know what to do," I muttered as silent tears streamed down my face.

"You should have told me." He turned away from the picture, bringing his fingers up to his head to massage his temples.

"I know."

"How long was it going on?" he finally asked.

"Three days before I met you," I said blankly. I was physically exhausted from holding anything back from him.

"Jesus, Landon," he heaved, and I heard the sob before it even came out of his mouth. I couldn't comfort him or hold him because I knew that is not what he wanted, so I let him cry by himself while I stood looking at the photograph.

"I did not know what to do," I repeated when he stopped crying.

"And you love her," he asked, but it was more of a statement than a question.

"In a different way than I love you," I said. He snorted in response but turned to face me. I panicked when I looked at him. That was the truth if I had ever said it. I loved the man I was looking at and the woman I had just left for the night. They made me complete in two different ways. I was whole with them and empty without them.

"I think I knew though," he said confidently as if he was trying to convince himself.

"What?"

"But I desperately wanted to believe otherwise," he said without losing his train of thought, "I knew that you did not get bug bites on your neck, but I wanted to believe that they were anything other than what I had originally asked. I think I would have preferred if you had told me that it was a dog bite." He laughed shakily as the tears subsided.

Oh my god, he laughed. This was going to be his final laugh with me. He was serving me. This was going to be his parting service; I waited there expecting total blame, disgust, anger, and confusion. I did not receive it. He kept talking, but I could not hear him because the last words he said had changed their tone. It was a tone that I did not warrant or deserve but desperately needed to hear. It released me from twenty years of hiding from myself, from everyone. His tone. *He changed my life. One person can change your life.*

Two people can change your life. How many would there have to be so this never happened again?

"Leo," I breathed.

"Let me finish," he said as his hands went back up to hold his head. "I honestly think it is a difference in age. I always forget how young you are because you don't act like twenty-one. There are certain things, traits, that come as you get older: confidence, work ethic, understanding, emotional control, memory...an ability to be who you are meant to be. That last one is the most important. Some people say that memories fade as you get older, but I think they simply change form. I often look back to when I was first becoming an adult and am embarrassed for myself when I think of things I said, or actions I did. It is quite humorous actually, but I realize that I am in no place to judge other people anymore. That's why I chose photography. I knew that I was different from a very early age and I found that people were constantly judging me for it. I wanted to search for difference, to capture it. To live it. I am not in a place to judge you right now because I can remember messing up in ways that are similar to how you fucked things up right now."

He paused.

"After she shook my hand and I left you, I was furious. I hope you really think deeply about that. That you remember these words I am saying…but do not feel them forever. I love you so much, and you broke a piece of my heart that had not belonged to you yet. You shattered what had belonged to you. It was irresponsible and you had no right to break it. I walked through all of my pictures – this whole gallery, my first big show – and hated every single one that was of you. I hated this show even though it was supposed to be one of the proudest moments of my life. Landon, it was my first big show. I thought about selling them and even went to the gallery director and told her that I was willing to put them on sale tonight. The only reason they did not immediately go on sale was because an anonymous donation had been received when the doors opened. It made everything profitable. I was not constrained by money. It was the first time in my life, I did not need to worry about it. I cannot even begin to process how odd that feeling is…"

Remy Mellac. *The love and protection of a parent*. Even if Sidonie had not told me that her father had donated to the gallery, I think I would have still known it was him. He orchestrated this for his daughter. He loved her by protecting her *while destroying me*.

"I have a bond with my photographs. To sell one is always sad for me and to not worry about parting with a single one, a single memory of you…that feeling Landon. I cannot even tell you. Anyways, it was late and she said that I should think about all the time and energy I had put into the gallery. I went back through all the rooms and still hated every single picture. Then I got caught in a conversation with the director for the Vogue shoot we did together. He came tonight with a whole group of other photographers and creatives. He found me and brought me to this picture. He asked me why the subject looked so familiar and I told him the truth. I told him that I had known you for much longer than I had let on. Do you know what he said?"

"No," I said, cutting off one of my sobs.

"He knew I was lying to everyone. That is why he came tonight. When he saw the very first test picture that morning, of you – standing there with your arms at your side, simply looking into the camera, looking at me – that there was an understanding. There was no lens separating us. Only people who know and love each other can convey so much emotion in such an ordinary pose. This is why he made you the center of that campaign. He combined you and I to make something greater. To sell that vision for the magazine, he knew that people needed to see what he had seen from that first picture."

"God," I sobbed, but I he was not finished.

"He told me that he had come tonight so he could offer me a contract. He wants to outsource the projects that he does not have time for, but thinks are original and noteworthy, things the public needs to see. He never shows up at gallery openings because he is too busy. He has people who report back to him. Then he said, and this is what really shocked me, that he also came tonight so he could see you."

"Me?"

"Yes. He came to see you behind the camera. He said that any artist who loves their subject so much, they would fill four rooms with pictures, is one in a million. Too many photographers try to fill their photos with their own style, their own personality, but only a few of them can take any moment and focus entirely on the subject, leaving themselves completely out of it. A photographer is never meant to be center stage. This is why he said I was special and different." Leo looked back at the beach photo, tears dragging down his high cheekbones.

"Why did he bring you to this picture out of all of the other ones?" I asked. It was the only semi-intelligent thing I could muster.

"He called this the weird picture. He said that it was different from all the others because there was a sense of uncertainty in it. He couldn't understand why Americans can smile and flip someone off so easily, so happily. Those two acts should not be together but you made them work." Leo laughed through a gargled sob and I found myself sigh in relief. Then he paused. "The whole reason I am telling you this is because you have to make a choice."

"What?"

"I am here for you if that is the choice you make. I love you. I will always love you, but I don't think that it is an unfair request to ask you to choose," he said blankly, and I shook my head as if that would help me understand what he was saying.

"What are you talking about?" I asked. The words did not click.

"My pride is hurt but I love you. It is simple to me and the simple things in life are what have brought me to where I am today. I know you are not an idiot. I know that you feel terrible about this. You are a human. You made this mistake but I can see you even if you cannot see yourself. I also know that regardless of what decision you make with me and her, this is something you will never do again, to anyone. In a way, I am helping myself, I am helping you, and I am helping someone else. That is why I do this. It is what motivates me every day."

"Oh my God." I wiped the tears from the corner of my eyes as my throat constricted for another time. This is not what I deserved; it is not what anyone deserved in the situation.

"I have one more thing to say before I go home."

"Okay." I looked at him expectantly.

"I don't want you making the choice for me. I will always be here for you even if we do not take another step together. You need to make this choice for yourself. There is never just one 'true love' in this life, as you have discovered. You should make this decision for yourself because in time I, or Sidonie, will have the opportunity to fall back in love. I have adored falling in love with you. Thank you."

He kissed me on the cheek before his steps followed him from the room.

The Product of March

I told her. I told her exactly what happened. We both cried in her apartment for what seemed like hours. There was no anger, no remorse, and no regret. In fact, she simply asked me to choose, just like Leo, because she loved me that much. I knew the choice I was going to make. That night, after I left her apartment, the night following my last day at the embassy, I withdrew my acceptance from Oxford University and paid a late-fee for my re-committal to Boston College. My dad paid the thousands of dollars without asking any questions and even had a business colleague call the university to confirm my spot.

"I will support you regardless of the financial cost," he said.

My mom applauded me for making the 'correct' decision. "It was never going to work anyway."

In the end, I knew that I could not chose either even though they had both had chosen me.

I informed them of my choice– Sidonie over lunch and Leo over dinner. I told each of them why I was not staying, and I cried with both of them after we agreed it was time for me to leave. Sidonie left me with a small kiss. I left her with a bracelet I had gotten for her in Copenhagen and a note that I had written for her.

Sidonie, I hope that you have done what you wish with your bracelet, but I hope you know how much I love you – that is the purpose of that note to you.

Leo stayed with me for the remainder of our meal together, and we held hands for the entire thing. I found myself crying at random times and he squeezed my hand to reassure me. He left me after the dinner. I wished him good luck with everything and presented him with a small box that I had made for him. He kissed me goodbye and then walked towards the cab.

Leonardo, I hope you kept the box. I am sorry I took a piece of your heart. In return, I tried to give you a symbolic representation of what you have of mine. Everything in there shows how much you mean to me and will hopefully remind you of our life-changing time together. I love you.

Then it ended. It was an end. There was no drama, no blowup, no crawling back to try to fix things. It ended. No one can prepare you for an end with so much closure, such a clean break. All ends I had ever experienced had a trail leading back to the beginning, tugging me closer so that beginning could ensnare me again. With them – Leo and Sidonie – I was left with everything and did not need to return to the start. It has closed. Time had stopped multiplying, compounding. The product of March had reached its full potential.

I turned to take a final walk through the park near my apartment after I had watched Leo step into his cab. He looked at me, smiled, and blew me a kiss. Then he got in the cab. I was back where I started the semester, but far ahead of where I began six months ago. I knew I was special. I didn't know just how special until March. Leo and Sidonie gave me everything I wanted. They filled in the parts of me that I never knew had been empty and filled in those parts that I did. The memories of them will be forever carved into the deepest parts of my soul because both of them helped unearth the things that make me special.

Maybe I will see them again, when I am the person they thought I was.

It is a funny thing – love – and I can say that only because I have experienced it. It is not an infatuation of two weeks where you cannot help but think about a person; in fact, I think it is the complete opposite. Regardless of the time we were apart, our relationship grew together in the absence of each other. They not only tolerated my faults, they truly saw that those faults were what made me human. In the span of six months, they did not change me – they made me human. To both of you, this is my thank you.

* * *

"Landon," Jake says, pulling me out of the reverie.

I give him a small smile and shake my head to clear the thoughts.

"That is my name," I say half-heartedly.

"Is everything okay?" he asks.

"It couldn't be better. What's up?"

"We are all going out for drinks now that all of us are moved in. I was thinking we could Uber into Boston? Everyone else is ready to go, we are just waiting on you."

I pull on my clothes, pile into the Uber, and then just twenty minutes later my roommates and I are all ordering our first legal drinks together since being back in the States. Everyone is so excited for this newfound freedom of drinking that I am not surprised when the second, third, and fourth round of drinks come.

"Landon, dude, you haven't said anything all night. We all saw what you were up to this summer. How the hell did you get a job in the embassy or wherever you were?" Danny scoffs, slugging his pilsner.

"Ah, yeah, one of the guys I met over there helped me get the job. It was an absolutely amazing experience living in Paris. My French got really good," I say, taking the last gulp of my fourth drink. The area around my eyes is already tingling.

"Yeah, that definitely gives us a lot of information," Nico laughs.

"What do you want to know?"

"You don't even know the life you live. What about all the traveling you did or the modeling? We saw your picture like all over the place in stores. You should be the one buying everyone the drinks," Matt jokes, jabbing my side.

"It all went really well. I was pretty surprised with the reception by all the photographers over there. I thought that I would have been too bulky for them and that I didn't have the look…I guess that wasn't the case." I shrug.

"Hold on…let me pull something up. I need to ask you about one picture," Sawyer says, scrolling through his phone. "Here. Tell me about this one. This looks like you are like ten years old."

I do not even need to see the picture before I know which one he was referring to. I had shared only one of Leo's pictures since I had left, and I was going to keep it like that. I was going to hold onto those moments forever, by myself with no outside opinion.

"That is probably my favorite photo of all time. I think it captures me in a really different light. The photographer was really special. He had this theory that there were three poses…"

"Okay, okay, well then what about the girls this summer?"

"Weren't you just asking about the picture?" I say to Sawyer. No one actually wants to hear my take– this is just a talking point to get me saying something.

"I think it's a great picture, don't get me wrong. But no offense dude, you look pretty gay in it," Sawyer says.

"Okay," Jake chimes in, and I see him glare at Sawyer.

"No," I laugh at Jake. "It's okay. Sawyer, I very much agree with you. I don't know if gay is the right word, but it certainly is more feminine than any of you are used to. One of the things I learned being in France was that there is definitely a spectrum of sexuality…"

"You are one of those people now?" Duncan yells from the other end of the table.

"One of what people?" I say defiantly.

"Those people that think that sex is a spectrum! Wow, France really did change you."

"I think the French and pretty much all of Europe is more comfortable in their sexuality than we are in the United States, so they don't feel these rigid roles that we do. I absolutely do think sex is a spectrum, but you have to be honest with yourself."

"I don't buy that shit for a second," Duncan says, and the table joins him in laughing again.

"You asked me about the picture and that was my answer," I mumble, irritated.

"What about the girls? Don't tell us you didn't hook up with anyone because I will not buy that for a second," Max insists, banging his fist on the table.

"I actually hooked up with only a few people while I was abroad. I don't know, I think the experience was more for me to find a few things out about myself."

"Like what? That you are on this spectrum?" Max laughs, trying to take another sip through breaths.

"Yes," I say concretely, and everyone turns to me. My face flushes bright red and my heartbeat jumps into my throat. This is a moment I have secretly been hoping for; if it didn't come tonight, I don't think it would come at all. I wait for what seems like an eternity, and then finally, Matt brakes the silence. Except he doesn't break it with a serious follow-up question– he breaks it with tears. He is laughing so hard that he begins to cry. Once Matt starts, everyone else starts laughing, and just like that my moment is over. My throat constricts and tears well in my eyes. No one else notices because everyone is now banging their glasses against the table, making an awful noise in the bar, tears streaming down their cheeks from uncontrolled laughter. It lasts for about one or two minutes, but by the time everyone settles down, I know that this will never be a conversation they will understand.

"Ah! Ah! Ah!" Max chortles, regaining control of himself as the contagious energy disperses into the air. "But really, tell us about the hookups. Were they foreign? Any models that we would know? The sex must have been bomb! Come on, give us something we can work with. You have barely said anything all night."

I tell them the truth.

"I fell in love this summer actually," I say, glancing over the rim of my glass. I know that with the number of drinks everyone has had, I am preaching to a lost cause.

"With who? Where was she from?" Nico says.

"I fell in love with two people actually," I spit out. "One was from Paris and the other was from Italy. Jake actually knows the girl from Paris. Most of you met Sidonie too. How can you not remember that? I brought her to Madrid." I glance at Jake.

"I do, that is right, but I don't know this girl from Italy. You never mentioned any girl from Italy...ever."

"It was more low-key than Sidonie, I think. I would have told you, but I guess I just didn't know how," I respond tiredly.

"What do you mean by that?" he asks, and his expression reveals that he is visibly hurt.

"How was the French girl?" Matt says.

"Hold on," Jake says to Matt and then leans in closer to me.

"Who was the Italian girl? Was she from Queen Mary? Was it that blonde girl?" he asks.

"Not quite," I say, shifting my attention back to Matt. I want to be completely honest with my best friend but do not think now was the perfect moment for a deep conversation with him. He deserves more respect and an explanation than that.

"Dude, you did not mention a single other person than Sidonie and the photographer."

"It wasn't a huge deal. It was kind of something I wanted to keep close to the chest," I say to the table though Jake has not moved on.

"Bullshit. You just said you fell in love with two people this summer and you have only told me about one of them. I didn't know you were hanging out with anyone except the girl from Paris and the photographer from Ita…" He trails off, his mouth left slightly open, and a blast of confusion hits his face. His eyes sparkle after what seems like an eternity and finally, he sees me. *This is worth everything.* My best friend, of years, had not seen me clearly before. Until now. *How sad; that is entirely my fault.* He loves me regardless of who I love.

He understands.

A different form of love than both Sidonie and Leo, Jakes love can also never be replicated and cannot be explained. It will merely be an understanding and a moment that will continue living as long as we both want it to. He knows me so well and knows exactly what I am saying. It's a rare and powerful moment to share a silent communication with someone about something so personal and profound.

"Jake?" Danny says, interrupting our conversation.

"I met her and she was beautiful. Uh yeah, the girl from Paris was one of those girls that you see in movies. I mean, I know a bunch of you essentially fell in love with Sidonie too! The perfect effortless ones, go figure. I, uh, also heard only snippets about the Italian one, but from what I can tell Landon is not lying about falling in love." He clears his throat. I see tears in his eyes too – happy tears, not laughing tears, and not sad tears.

"And?" Matt says after a minute of silence. "Wow, this whole London thing must have really changed you two. What is going on tonight?"

"Maybe Landon should tell you himself, if you are open to actually listening to him, not just berating him. They did more traveling together than the two of us did. I can say that the girl from Paris is someone who you only meet once in your life though," Jake says, draining his drink while everyone returns their attention to me.

"I don't know where to begin," I say smiling, and then recount a few stories from my summer with both Leo and Sidonie using gender neutral pronouncs. Everything is so raw that by the end of the night everyone at the table, as well as the people eavesdropping at the table next to us, are crying, laughing, moaning, and smiling – sliding back and forth on the emotional spectrum. My only wish is for all these guys, people I love and wish the best for, to find something like this in their lives. Most people don't ever find someone, I understand that now, but I pray that everyone at least gets a chance.

* * *

"I am so ready for this year!" Sawyer says, stumbling back into our Mod after we arrive back on campus.

"Sawyer, you do that big guy. Got to get bigger though– your legs are looking a little weak these days," I joke.

"Shut up! I am going to pull so many freshman girls this year with these muscles." He flexes his arms and legs before slumping into the couch.

His comment transports me back to Saint Patrick's Day, standing on that sidewalk outside of Jake's LSE dorm room as we walked to find Waxy O'Connors.

I had said that same exact thing.

"I don't feel the need to pull freshman girls this year. Do you, Landon?" Jake says, smiling at me.

"Oh God, I don't know if I can handle anyone this year!" I laugh before heading upstairs.

* * *

I wanted this to have a happy ending, so I gave it one. This love may not have been long-term but it transcended time. This story did not end as a fairy tale but the memory is still as vivid and fresh now as the day I met each one of them. A photograph— cleanly lit and set on full display.

My March compounded on itself. I started with nothing and, magically, one was added. That one became two and as I sat at that table in Boston, months after it was finished, I was more whole, one hundred times more whole, even though I was a thousand miles away from the original two. The product was greater than the sum of the parts. That is my happy ending; I felt loved and gave love. I have spent years writing and rewriting this last paragraph. I am not a real author; I am just somebody who wants to remember love.

Here are my final words for those who want to live; there comes a point in life when rock-bottom becomes the normal even if you do not know you are at rock-bottom, rejection becomes reality, families break apart, friends move away, work drains your energy, and when the absence of human connection, regardless of its form, is so great that you feel physically empty and hungry. Our "dream job" becomes more of an impediment than fulfilling, the family that we took for granted slowly disperses, and the time we wanted to speed up is now moving too fast.

For most human beings, our greatest weakness is not appreciating the moment we are living. There is beauty in everything, but most of us do not come to that realization until we are on our deathbed. This is life. Life adds upon itself and very frequently compounds.

Let it happen.

I urge you to look back and appreciate the memories and people who have created the person you see in the mirror. If you can do this, then you will understand that you are no longer empty. You can begin your ascent from rock-bottom but must first start climbing; it takes inner strength, clear disclosure, and a will to climb to get back to who you want to be and how you want to live. At the end of the day, it takes one nanosecond to change your life: Whether you are standing in the dark outside of a subway station as spring breathes the first signs of life into your surroundings or shifting on the sticky floors of a college dive bar, my hope is that each of you let these special moments happen because there will be great joy in watching them grow.

Why should we deprive ourselves of those things that make us special?